Also by Rob Edwards

Holiday Novellas:
Seven Tails of Christmas - A Christmas Novella
Life at 24 Frames Per Second - A New Year's Novella

Threads of Life:
Prisons - A Novel
Coming Soon - I Do or I Don't

The Friendship Effect

Rob Edwards

For Dayna Marie

Edwards

1

Friday before Thanksgiving

"What are you thankful for, Dad?"

My daughter's words barely registered at the back of my brain. I was stuck in my usual breakfast position—forehead resting on the palm of my left hand, fingers combed into my red hair, my eyes staring down at my cell phone on the table, taking in the day's stock projections. As the CEO of a bank, I clung to the stock reports. At any given time, they could be my lifeline or my kryptonite.

I held a cup of coffee in my right hand, which was half-full but already cold. In between the phone and the cup was a small plate that contained a scrambled egg, also cold, and butter-soggy toast that had three bites out of each. I couldn't tell you the last time I actually ate a warm breakfast.

"Earth to Dad!"

Somehow the words finally reached my ears and my out-of-body stock journey concluded abruptly. "What's up?" I looked up and took a sip of coffee.

My daughter, Amber rolled her eyes the way teenagers do when they want to show you how completely uncool you are, and how they're doing all they can just to tolerate you. "I just told you. I have a paper due today, and it has to be something about Thanksgiving. So I wanted to know what you're thankful for." She had a notebook next to her cereal bowl, hand clutching a pink gel pen, ready to write.

"What I'm thankful for?"

She rolled her eyes once more. "Yes."

I was still trying to clear the ups and downs of the market report out of my head when the reality of what she said finally sank in. "Wait. You have a paper due *today*, and you're just starting it at breakfast?"

"Oh my God. *Dad*, you're not being helpful."

I sat my coffee cup down and looked over at my daughter. "You watched a movie with your mother last night. I was working in the den, and I heard her ask you if you were all set for school today, and you told her you were."

Amber shrugged. "I was. I knew I could count on my father at breakfast to help me finish my paper, and everything would be fine. But since you're now letting me down..."

Now it was my turn to roll my eyes. I love how teenagers can turn things on a dime and make it your fault that bad things are happening to them. Rather than argue with her, I thought it best to let experience be her tutor today. I picked up my coffee cup, raised it to her in a cheer, and downed the last bit of bitter liquid. Then I smacked my lips, satisfied, and said, "I'm thankful there is coffee on Friday mornings."

Grabbing the crutches that I had leaning against the counter behind me, I hoisted myself out of my chair. Since my left leg was amputated when I was nine years old, my empty left pant leg hung down, swaying about. I winked at my daughter. "Good luck with that paper."

"Dad, don't go," Amber begged. "I need you to be serious."

Slipping the phone in my side pocket, I shuffled over to her. "I am. The coffee thing is called an angle." I kissed her on the forehead. "Nobody else will have that in their paper. You'll get points for originality."

She did that other thing teenagers do: a combination of a sigh and a growl all in one exhale. But somehow, I was very satisfied with my answer.

My wife Margo strolled into the kitchen, hair pulled back, dressed in her black leggings and Buckeyes sweatshirt ready for her morning jog. She had an unusually buoyant spring in her step.

"Hey, babe." I kissed her and straightened my tie. "I need you to be ready for our daughter to redo her senior year."

She just looked back at me and grinned.

"What?" I asked.

Margo turned and grabbed a mug from its hanger under the cupboard and walked to the coffee pot. "I'm just excited about tonight."

One of the things I hated the most was when Margo scheduled things and then acted like I should know about them. Several times I had made other plans, which of course I would have to cancel. But the other part of that equation is that, because of my career, my mind is filled with stock reports, and she actually does tell me things that I completely forget until it's time to go. But I have learned the correct question to ascertain which of these scenarios is correct. "What's tonight again?"

She spun around and narrowed her eyes at me. "Kenneth Ronald Pritchard, don't you dare tell me you forgot that we are meeting Casey and Celine at the club tonight for dinner because they have news they want to share with us."

It was the latter. The system worked to perfection once again. I nodded. "Oh, yeah. The news."

9

Margo set down her cup, put her arms around my neck, and kissed me lightly. She giggled. "We're going to be grandparents."

"Don't jump to conclusions," I said, sliding my crutches to the side. Margo stepped back to let me pass.

"What else could it be?" she said, grabbing the coffee pot and pouring herself a cup.

I crutched my way to the front door and sat down in the chair that was placed there for me to use when I was ready to leave the house. There was also a thin metal left leg wearing a dress shoe leaning against the wall. "I don't know, but given our son's penchant for big ideas and no follow-through, it could be anything. It doesn't necessarily mean grandchildren." I leaned the crutches against the wall and slid my left pant leg up to reveal a pin sticking out of the sock at the end of my thigh where long ago, my knee once was.

Margo followed me out of the kitchen with her fresh cup of coffee. "Well, you'll have to forgive the silly dreams of a wanna-be grandmother."

I grabbed the prosthesis leaning against the wall, slid the cupped end over my thigh, and pushed until I heard the sharp click which told me it was attached securely. Then I pushed my dress pants down over the metal limb and stood on my own two feet.

"They aren't silly dreams, my love. When that day actually comes, I know you'll be the best grandmother in the history of grandmothers." I kissed her once more, grabbed a coat off the rack, and threw it on. Then I reached for the car keys.

"Remember I need the Escalade today," Margo said. "You have to take the Mini Cooper."

This was another one of those memory moments. I looked back at her and asked the proper question. "Why am I taking the Mini again?"

Margo swallowed her sip of coffee. "Ken, you aren't

remembering anything lately. The ladies and I are doing lunch, and then we have that big load of pillows and blankets to drop off at the children's wing at the hospital."

Again, it was scenario number two. Now that she mentioned it, I remember her telling me about it a few days ago. I nodded. "Sorry, honey. I've slept since then." I grabbed the keys to the Mini Cooper out of the ceramic bowl on the stand next to the front door, slipped my laptop case over my shoulder, and stepped out into the brisk November morning.

Isabel Alejandro, our housekeeper, was coming up the front steps with her usual over-friendly smile. Isabel was always pleasant, no matter what was going on in the world. "Good morning, Mr. Pritchard." She held a paper bag in front of me. "I brought a batch of Emilia's churros for breakfast. They're freshly made and still warm."

I could smell them, which made me want to turn around and go back in for a second cup of coffee. Emilia was Isabel's sister and a fantastic cook. Her churros were terrific, but her huevos rancheros was legendary. I was practically heartbroken to have to go. "I'm sorry, Isabel," I said, sadly waving off the offer. "I just finished breakfast. But please make sure Margo and Amber save me one."

"I will do that, Mr. Pritchard. Have a very good day."

"Thank you. You too, Isabel." I didn't have Isabel's cheer, but I was able to at least be cordial to her after one cup of coffee.

I definitely did not like driving the Mini Cooper — not because it was a bad car. In fact, it was a great car. It's just that it was difficult to get my prosthesis in. I had to manually pull my leg in, which I was willing to do for Margo when duty called. I could slide right into the Cadillac Escalade without any issue.

I pulled out of the driveway and drove off, the echo of Amber's question was still ringing through my head. *What am I thankful for?* To be honest, it wasn't really the question that took me by surprise, it was the fact that I couldn't come up with an answer right away. And that fact alone seems ironic since I had the choice of driving a Mini Cooper or a Cadillac Escalade from my very nice house in Upper Arlington, one of the nicest suburbs of Columbus, to my prestigious job at Ohio Continental Bank—in fact, I was the first disabled CEO in bank history. I had a fantastic marriage. Margo was everything I could have ever asked for in a wife. She was beautiful, kind, supportive, a great mother, and truth be told, I still couldn't believe my luck that she ever agreed to marry me. I had two great kids. Sure, they could be…kids at times, but they were still great and I'm very proud of them.

It wasn't because I was disabled. I've dealt with prosthetic legs for so long it's not even a thing I even think about anymore.

I should be able to point to any one of those things and say I'm extremely grateful. But for some reason, there was something gnawing at me. When Amber asked the question at the breakfast table, I didn't have an answer. So I said the first thing that came to my mind. If I hadn't had a cup of coffee in my hand at that moment, I probably would still be trying to come up with something.

It was certainly not that I was unhappy, and I didn't have issues with depression. I considered myself happy, even with all of the extra added stress of the leadership helm I had been given. I felt I was handling the pressure well, but each day seemed increasingly tough to get through, and I really didn't look forward to heading into work like I used to. I wasn't crazy about the idea of a countdown clock to retirement like I saw with so many others. That day was at least fifteen years away, and I didn't want to have to wait that long to look forward to getting out of bed again.

I wound through the thick Columbus traffic. One of the first things I did after I was hired was switch my office to the main branch building downtown instead of the glass and steel structure out in Whitehall much to the chagrin of the board, who loved to micromanage my daily activities and decisions.

I pulled into the underground parking garage and to my reserved spot next to the elevator. I lifted my left leg out of the car, slid my laptop case over my shoulder, and pulled myself free from the clutches of the Mini Cooper. I had the option to take the elevator all the way to the tenth floor where my office was located, but I always chose to get off at the first floor and walk across the main floor to the elevators in the back of the building instead. The employees weren't fond of my pass-throughs. I think it was stressful having the CEO visit them every day like I was checking up on them or something. The noisy bustle of a bank getting ready to open in the morning always grew a little quieter when I entered. But I still loved it. There was something elegant about the wooden interior of the old bank, and the fresh energy of a new day in a financial institution that I found thrilling.

The employees often stopped and stared when I walked by. I was so used to walking with my prosthesis that I had very little limp, so it wasn't that. I knew their nickname for me was, "Long Ken Ginger." I'd heard the bank manager came up with that one. Perhaps he felt my move to the branch was a bit of a pirate's move or something. Or maybe he just felt compelled to make cracks at my expense. It was a part of life that a disabled person got used to. And if I'm being honest, the Long Ken Ginger one was probably the most creative I'd heard yet.

I took the elevator to the tenth floor and stepped out into the lobby where my assistant, Dianne Weathers, was seated. I waved and was about to say good morning, but before the words came out of my mouth, she pointed to my office. "Mr. Byers is waiting for you."

Carl Byers was the new chairman of the OCB Board of Directors, and I couldn't necessarily count him as a fan.

I stopped in my tracks, took a breath, and thought a

moment. Did I want to go through that door into my office or did I want to go back down to the bank floor and hang out with my really good friends? But being the CEO means you are required to face the music. I nodded my thanks to Dianne and forged on in to see Carl standing by the window, hands in his pockets, watching the sun rise over Columbus.

"Good morning, Mr. Chairman. What can I do for you today?" I said, trying to channel Isabel's pleasantness.

Carl turned and nodded at me. "Pritchard. Good morning. I came to see you over a few concerns from the board."

Carl was a tall man. He had to be at least 6'8. He always looked down on me, literally and figuratively. He was dressed in a brown suit, with a charcoal-colored shirt and brown tie. Never had I seen clothes more suited for a man's disposition. I set my laptop case on the floor, gestured to one of the large leather chairs in front of my desk, and removed my coat. "Sure. Have a seat. I'll get us some coffee."

"No need. I'll not take much time." Carl sat in the chair and crossed his legs.

"Okay." I draped my coat over the back of my chair and sat down to face my adversary. "What seems to be the concern?"

"It's not just one concern," Carl said, linking his fingers together in front of him. "It's pretty much how you're running our banks. Everything from lowering interest rates on loans to the investment choices you're making."

"My investment choices?"

"The bottom line here, Ken," Carl looked down and brushed a piece of lint off his lapel, "is that we have received several calls from stockholders disgruntled about their shrinking dividend checks."

I took a breath to give me a second before I spoke. "That must be very frustrating for everyone, but you hired me to put an ailing financial institution back on solid ground. The decisions I'm making are doing that."

"Let's be clear. I didn't want to hire you," Carl said. "I voted against you. I wanted Adam Akers, who I think you are aware, landed the Indiana Federal position, and the word is that his stockholders are very happy with the way their dividend checks are growing."

"I am very aware of Akers and his recklessness with Forex trading."

"High risk, high reward. It beats the lifeless commodities that you're jumping on all the time."

"Those lifeless commodities are insured against loss, thus protecting the bank's assets and the stockholder's investments. Forex isn't."

Carl shifted his weight and draped his arm over the back of the chair to look as pompous as his attitude. "If you're not confident enough in your trading skills to know when to take the risks well…"

He let that line trail off to let me fill in the rest and let my self-doubt run rampant in my head. What he didn't realize was that I didn't have any self-doubt. So I thought I'd show him. "There are whispers in the wind that the Fed is considering raising interest rates. That will put Akers' risky money plays in the hole, all the while solidifying my investments and putting your bank on even more stable ground. Will that make our stockholders happy?"

"I haven't heard of any interest rate increase by the Feds."

"Well, it's not really your job to be in the know. That's why you hired me." I leaned back and crossed my arms to look as confident as I sounded. "Is there anything else I can do for you, Carl?"

Carl uncrossed his legs and leaned forward. "How about handing me your letter of resignation?"

That was it. The real reason he came here. Just like any bully, when he realized he couldn't shake my confidence, he had to get rougher. I'd forced him to reveal his long-term. But I learned long ago to never let anyone see me get rattled.

There's no way a disabled person could become a CEO if they didn't appear ten times more confident as someone who was not disabled. I shook my head. "I'm sorry Carl. It's going to take a vote from the entire board to get me out of here."

"Well," Carl slapped his knees and stood. "I guess we'll see you Monday after Thanksgiving then." He smiled and walked toward the door. "Have a good holiday, Pritchard." Having revealed his entire plan to lobby the board against me, he let the door slam behind him.

I unzipped my case and pulled out the first thing I often needed when I entered my office—my bottle of ibuprofen. My workday headache had already started and ibuprofen was my drug of choice, especially since Tylenol doesn't work for redheads. I popped the top, poured out two pills, tossed them in my mouth, and swallowed. I looked in the bottle and was stressed to find I only had five pills left. I needed to get more. A full bottle of ibuprofen always made me feel more secure somehow. I put the top on the bottle and threw it back into my case, then I pulled out my laptop and jammed it onto the dock. As soon as the monitor lit up, I typed in my password and went straight to Bloomberg. com. I clicked and flipped through the headlines looking for any word on the Federal Reserve. If there's one thing I did have it was a solid sense of the market. We'd been in a bullish state long enough that I was fairly confident we'd soon hear rumblings about rising interest rates. But what I'd told Carl was a lie. I hadn't heard anything yet. I picked up my phone and hit Dianne's number.

"Yes?"

"Is he gone?"

"The elevator doors just closed."

"Have you heard anything recently about the Fed adjusting interest rates?"

"No. Nothing, but I can look. Why?"

I shook my head while I stared into my monitor.

"Because I just bluffed my butt off in here, and I'm hoping it doesn't come back to bite me."

"I'll keep my eyes out for anything."

"Thanks, Dianne." I hung up the phone realizing that Dianne's loyalty was something I was definitely thankful for. But expressing that as the answer to Amber's question at the breakfast table, that I was very thankful for another woman's loyalty, wouldn't have gone over too well.

The phone rang before I could even look back at my monitor. It was Ryan Reed, the president of OCB. He was always good for a laugh. I picked it up, and the conversation began the way it always did in the fall, "My poor Browns. Did you see that debacle yesterday?"

I had to laugh. He hung his hat on the Cleveland Browns. "Did you go to the game?"

"Of course." Ryan was a season ticket holder with seats just off the 50-yard line.

We chuckled back and forth about football and life before getting to work. He updated me on policy changes that were up for discussion at our Zoom meeting with the bank managers at 11:00. It was always good to talk to Ryan. We'd been friends for years, and he was one of the few people that made the job at least halfway enjoyable.

After Ryan and I finished up, I spent the next hour rabbit-trailing through Bloomberg before the Zoom meeting with the branches. The meeting took me to noon when Dianne knocked at the door to deliver my #12, my standing sandwich order from Jimmy John's. I closed my laptop to eat at my desk. One problem with moving my office to the branch was that there was no one to eat lunch with. Nobody wanted to be the one to make friends with the big guy; it smacked too much of brown-nosing. So, I ate alone in my office nearly every day.

But my lunch was interrupted by Dianne ringing me. "Mr. Pritchard, there's an Emilia Alejandro out here who says she's a friend of yours and is insisting she speak with you."

"Emilia? Ahhh." I dropped my sandwich and wiped my mouth. I heard chatter in the background and Dianne spoke again. "Apparently there is an issue with a loan application."

I wiped a drop of mayo off my hand. "Sure, go ahead and send her in." I wrapped up the other half of my sandwich and the door to my office swung open. Emilia burst in with a bank employee on her heels, looking nervous. "Hello, Mr. Pritchard. Thank you for helping me." She pointed to the man behind her. "This fool didn't know you and I are friends."

The man stood in front of my desk, clutching papers, looking anxiously around the room.

I stood and held out my hand. "Hi there. Ken Pritchard."

The man smiled. "Nice to meet you, Mr. Pritchard. I'm Steve Paxton." He then realized my hand was hanging out, and he awkwardly shook it.

"Did you get the churros I sent over this morning?" Emilia asked me.

"Oh, no. Isabel brought them, but I had already eaten breakfast. I told her to save me one though."

"Good for you," Emilia said pointing her finger at me. "You will like them. It was an excellent batch."

I nodded, then looked over at Paxton. "What seems to be the trouble?"

"Oh. Yes. Ummm..." He placed the papers he was holding on my desk.

"This guy tells me he can't give me the money to start my Mexically Cafe," Emilia said. "I said I knew you, and that we would get this thing straightened out."

"Well let's take a look." I nodded at the chairs. "Please have a seat."

I sat and looked over the papers. It was quickly clear why he had been telling Emilia what she didn't want to hear. "Emilia, it says the only collateral you are willing to put down is your car."

18

Emilia shrugged. "It's all I have. But my son is a co-signer."

I flipped a page to see the co-signators. "But he is currently a part-time mechanic."

"Yes, but he is taking business classes at night. He will be running the business side, and I will do the cooking," she said with a proud smile.

I pointed at the paperwork. "So, the person you have co-signing won't even be making the kind of money you wrote down here?"

Emila frowned. "No. But like I just said, he will be helping me run the business. We are all very serious about this."

I sighed.

"Mr. Pritchard? Is there a problem?" she asked.

"Emilia," I looked up at her and tapped the application with my finger while I thought of the right words to say. "This is what we, in the banking business, call a bad investment."

Emilia jumped from her chair. "I am *not* a bad investment. You have tasted my cooking. You know I can do this."

I sat back and put up my hands. "Your cooking is unbelievable, Emilia. I have no doubt you would gain a following," I said. "The problem is you can't use your cooking skills as collateral and the bank absolutely requires collateral."

"So, what are you saying?"

I looked back at the papers in front of me and shook my head. "I had my boss in here this morning telling me he was searching for a reason to fire me. I think if I signed these papers it would be just the thing he'd need to make it happen." I looked back up at her. "I'm so sorry, Emilia. I can't approve this loan. But perhaps you can get a job as a cook in…"

Emilia screamed something in Spanish and slammed the

door behind her. What was it with slamming doors today?

Paxton stood and nodded. "I'm very sorry for the interruption, Mr. Pritchard. If I could just…" He pointed at the papers.

"Oh, sure." I handed the application to him. "Thanks for all the hard work, Steve."

Paxton nodded back, smiled, scurried to the door, and closed it very quietly when he left.

I spun my chair around and looked out the window at the world busying itself. How many more frustrated people were out there who I couldn't help?

Just then my phone buzzed in the pocket of my suit coat. I pulled it out to see Todd Harter's name on the screen. He was an old school buddy of mine that I hadn't spoken to in years. Todd was the guy who seemed to keep in touch with everyone from school—not just high school, but middle school and elementary school, too. And not just the students. He knew all the teachers and principals and secretaries and what was going on with everyone at any time. Something must be going down for him to be calling. I hit the button. "Hey, Todd. It's been a while."

"Hey, Ken. I just found something out and thought I'd better give you a call."

"What's up?"

"I don't know if you heard or not, but Bobby Booker is in hospice care."

"Bobby Booker?" That was a name from the distant past.

"Yeah. I knew you and Bobby were really tight for a minute back in the day, So, I thought you'd want to know."

Suddenly, the realization of what Todd had said hit me between the eyes. "Bobby Booker's in *hospice*? What happened?"

"Some type of cancer, I guess. I'll text you his address and phone number. He's still living down by Cincinnati if you want to see him."

"Huh," I said, shaking my head trying to put it all in

perspective. "Okay, thanks, Todd."

"No problem. Take care, Ken."

"You, too." I tapped off the call and looked back out the window. That was definitely a name I hadn't expected to hear today, or any other day for that matter. "Bobby Booker," I said aloud. It was the name of someone from long ago—someone I'd hated, then loved, then forgot about completely.

Edwards

2

Back in the Day

The first day of fifth grade could be unpleasant for any short, red-haired kid. But for Kenny Pritchard it was terrifying. This was not only his first day of school, it was his first day of school with a prosthetic leg.

Kenny had gotten a knee infection the previous May and missed the last two weeks of fourth grade. He also missed the Memorial Day weekend his parents had planned on the island of Put-In-Bay—a place Kenny always loved because only bikes and golf carts were allowed on the island, and Kenny's dad always let him drive when nobody was on the back trails.

But the infection had not been discovered in time, so the doctors took "extreme measures." Now Kenny was left ambling along awkwardly, like the zombie people from the Vincent Price movie *The Last Man on Earth*.

His father had been nice enough to drop Kenny off on

the first day of school, instead of making him walk the three blocks on his new prosthetic leg. He stopped the car in the lot behind the buses and put it in park. "Look at all the kids so excited. It's got to feel good to be back."

Kenny watched the stream of kids coming off the buses and gathering around the front of the school. They were laughing, running, talking, but all he wanted to do was crawl in the back seat and hide.

"Go ahead, son. Go enjoy your day."

Kenny looked up at his dad. "Can't I just go to work with you? I promise I'll be quiet."

Kenny's father chuckled. "I'm sure all those kids are just as nervous as you are. You'll be fine." He reached over and opened Kenny's door for him. "Now, go have fun."

With a pout, Kenny grabbed his *Land of the Lost* lunch box and slid out of the green Buick Estate wagon.

"Have a great day, son." Kenny's dad said with a smile.

Continuing to pout, Kenny used his hand and his hip to shut the massive door, which closed with a creak and a clunk. His father waved, then drove around the buses and out of the parking lot. Kenny turned and headed toward the gathering mass of kids, shifting his weight with each step to pull the heavy prosthetic leg forward.

The other kids ignored him, which suited Kenny just fine. But then one loud voice cut through all the chatter like a hot knife through cotton candy, "Hey look. It's Peg-Leg Pete!" That was one voice Kenny did not need to hear thirty seconds into his first day of school.

The group of students quieted and parted to reveal Bobby Booker, a former fourth-grade troublemaker. How he made it to fifth grade Kenny couldn't understand. But there he stood, with his trouble-sights aimed directly at Kenny.

Bobby was close to a head taller than his classmates and nearly twice as wide. He had dark blond hair that looked like it had never come in contact with a comb, and a face that looked like someone spilled a box full of freckles. He stood pointing at Kenny and laughing, surrounded by his group of loyal followers: Sawyer, Gable, and Tunney. Kenny referred to them as The Bookees.

"How does it feel to be Frankenstein?" Bobby stuck his arms out straight, stiffened his limbs, and stomped around growling, "I'm Pritchard-Stein. Grrrrr."

On cue, the Bookees laughed as if they were paid to.

Kenny scowled, dropped his head, and moved to walk past them, but Bobby caught his arm and yanked him back. "Where ya, goin,' weirdo?"

Kenny stumbled backward, nearly falling. "I'm going to the classroom." He took a step forward but Bobby stepped in his way and blocked his path. Then the three Bookees surrounded him, leaving him nowhere to go. Since he was shorter, Kenny stood there and looked straight at the second from the top button on Bobby's green and yellow striped rugby shirt.

"Go ahead. Try and go to the classroom now."

He didn't want to look the bear in the eye so he let his gaze drop to his Keds sneakers, hoping the jerks surrounding him would get bored and walk away.

"Watcha lookin' at loser?"

Kenny silently wished for a miracle—that his father had forgotten to tell him something and would drive up, see what was going on, and spank Bobby in front of everybody.

No such luck. Bobby smacked at Kenny's lunchbox, knocking it out of his left hand onto the ground. It popped open and his bologna sandwich and bag of Fritos fell out at Tunney's feet. The oaf, a short guy no taller than Kenny, laughed and stomped on them, smashing the sandwich into mush and popping the bag of Fritos, sending corn chip crumbs everywhere.

Kids were crowding in now, watching everything that was going on. Kenny felt like crying, but he knew that would be the worst thing he could possibly do. So, he just continued to look at his shoes.

"I said, whatcha lookin' at?" Bobby pushed him and he fell back into Sawyer, who was nearly as tall as Bobby and just as smelly. Sawyer caught him, laughed, and shoved him forward again.

That was it. That was all Kenny wanted to take. He looked directly at Bobby's freckled face.

"Leave me alone, Bobby Booger!" He couldn't believe that those words actually came out of *his* mouth. It was like a ventriloquist moment—like somebody used their own voice to make it look and sound like he'd said it. But no. He *had* said it. It was out there. And Bobby didn't look too happy about it.

The rest of the kids standing around all shouted "Oooohhhhh," the way that they do when they know someone is about to get pounded into the dirt. Even the Bookees took a few steps back.

Bobby said nothing more. He gritted his teeth, balled up his fist, and hit Kenny squarely in the chest, knocked the wind out of him, and sent him sprawling backward onto the ground gasping for breath. Kenny rolled over onto his stomach to try to get up, but Bobby leaned in and hit him twice in the back. Then Bobby kicked Kenny's wooden prosthetic leg. It didn't hurt him, though. Instead, it was Bobby who cried out in pain.

The kids around them were all jumping up and down and shouting, "Fight, fight, fight!" But it was certainly *not* a fight. Kenny was just hoping to survive.

Bobby reached down, grabbed Kenny's left foot, and yanked, trying to take the leg away from him, but his leg was fastened to his thigh with leather straps and metal buckles. It wasn't coming off. Bobby dragged Kenny along the ground by his leg, and the crowd of kids parted to let Bobby through. Kenny tried to wiggle out of his clutches, searching the ground for anything to hold onto, grabbing at the grass, which he pulled out in clumps.

Suddenly Bobby stopped, and the crowd went completely quiet.

Kenny looked up. The Bookees and the rest of the kids were were staring, too, with wide eyes and open mouths at something above him. It was painful, but Kenny pulled himself up to see what everyone was looking at. Mr. Fenstamaker, the principal, towered above him with his hands on his hips like an angry Green Giant. He glared down on Bobby through his square, black-framed glasses. He reminded Kenny of Frankenstein with a short flat-topped haircut.

Bobby let go of Kenny's leg, and it dropped to the ground with a thump.

Mr. Fenstamaker was flanked by the much shorter and plumper Mrs. Walters, the assistant principal, who always had her dyed brown hair formed into what looked like a very stiff and quite unmovable short tower above her head. She looked at the situation with a sadly disappointed expression on her face.

Mr. Fenstamaker grabbed Bobby by the ear. "Mrs. Walters, would you please take Kenny to the office and make sure he's not hurt?"

"Certainly, Mr. Fenstamaker."

Mr. Fenstamaker dragged Bobby away, who protested very little except for the occasional, "Ahh, ahhh, ahhh!" because it was most certainly painful to be pulled along by your ear. Kenny fought the urge to cheer.

"Okay, kids," Mrs. Walters said to the throng of students who had gathered around to watch the morning's entertainment. "Off to class with you. Hurry, before the bell rings."

The kids all wandered off and Mrs. Walters knelt down next to Kenny. "Are you okay, son?' Is your leg still attached?"

Kenny rolled over and sat up. He felt the straps on his thigh. They hadn't moved an inch. He nodded.

"Can I help you up?" She held out a hand and Kenny took it. She carefully lifted him off the ground and brushed the dirt off his shirt and trousers. "You have a little grass stain on your pants. Just tell your mother to scrub it with a toothbrush and white vinegar before she throws it into the wash, and it will come right out."

Kenny nodded again, and Mrs. Walters picked up his now-empty lunch box. She put the smashed sandwich and the empty Fritos bag in it, took his hand, and escorted him into the school. Welcome back signs with bright suns, trees, squirrels and bunnies, cut out of colored construction paper, were plastered over all of the bulletin boards in the hallway. Students were rushing to their classrooms, many of them glancing over at him to see if he was crying or not. Kenny wouldn't give them the satisfaction.

Mrs. Walters walked him into the office. Bobby Booker was sitting in a chair, rubbing his ear. He avoided looking at Kenny as they passed by.

Kenny was escorted right into Mrs. Walters' office, and she closed the door behind her. "Have a seat right here, hon." She pointed to one of the yellow vinyl seats she had along one wall in her office. Kenny ambled over and sat heavily into the chair.

She opened his lunchbox and threw his sandwich and chip bag in the trash. Then she grabbed her purse from an open desk drawer and pulled a dollar out of it. She walked over and stuffed the dollar in his pants pocket. "This will take care of lunch today." She sat in the chair next to him.

"Are you hurt at all? Anything I need to put a Band-Aid on?"

Kenny shook his head His lower lip quivered and tears started to leak out of his eyes.

"Oh, honey. I know." She put her arms around him and hugged him gently. "Kids can be so damn rotten sometimes."

The door opened and Mr. Fenstamaker stepped in.

"Is he all right?"

She sat Kenny back and nodded. "Just a little shook up is all."

"Fine." Mr. Fenstamaker jerked his thumb toward another door. "Bring him into my office before we send him to his classroom."

"Will do."

Mr. Fenstamaker walked out, leaving the door open. He stopped in front of Bobby and pointed to his doorway. "Let's go, young man."

"Are you ready to go in, too?" Mrs. Walters asked.

Kenny was afraid and also confused. Why did *he* have to go into the principal's office? Wasn't he the victim here? It didn't seem fair. "But why? I didn't do anything?"

"He knows that," Mrs. Walters said, rubbing his shoulder. "He just wants to get the whole story." She patted his back. "Come on. Let's get you in there."

The last thing Kenny wanted today or ever was to be inside the same room with Bobby Booker. But it looked like he had no choice. He let Mrs. Walters take him by the hand and lead him through the main area into Mr. Fenstamaker's office. It was spacious with a huge desk and a big round table off to the side with chairs around it. There were also yellow vinyl chairs along the opposite wall, which was where Bobby was sitting. Kenny wondered why there was so much seating in the principal's office. How many kids could possibly get into trouble at one time?

Mrs. Walters pulled out a chair from the table for Kenny. It had a wooden back and seat with chrome metal legs—not as comfortable looking as the yellow vinyl chairs, but Kenny wasn't going to complain if it meant that he didn't have to sit next to Bobby, who smelled even more stinky than usual.

Mr. Fenstamaker sat behind his desk, a serious-looking scowl on his face. "Thank you, Mrs. Walters. Please close the door on your way out."

Mrs. Walters nodded, smiled at Kenny, and gave him

another reassuring pat on the back before backing out of the room and closing the door quietly.

Kenny looked at Mr. Fenstamaker, who was twirling a pen in his hand and looking back and forth from Bobby to Kenny. He finally dropped it on the desk and stood. "So, Bobby." He walked around and sat back on his desk directly in front of Bobby and crossed his arms. "Can you tell me why it's so fun to pick on someone who has a disability?"

Bobby lowered his hand from his aching ear and put his head down.

"I asked you a question, young man. I want an answer," Mr. Fenstamaker said loudly.

Bobby jumped, startled at the anger in the man's voice. "No, sir. I can't tell you why I did it. I don't have a good reason."

Mr. Fenstamaker turned to Kenny. "Can you tell me how all this started?"

Kenny shivered as if a cold wind blew through the room. Saying a single word would put a target on his back for the rest of his life. How could this man be asking him this in front of the enemy?

"I can't remember," Kenny mumbled, shaking his head.

Mr. Fenstamker looked back at Bobby. "You know I can't tolerate this kind of behavior, right?"

Bobby nodded.

Mr. Fenstamaker sighed. "You're suspended for two weeks. I'll call your father to come pick you up."

"Please, no!" Bobby jumped out of his seat like a torch was lit under his butt. "Please don't tell my Dad." Bobby burst into tears. "I'm sorry, Mr. Fenstamaker. I'll do whatever you want. I'm really sorry. *Please* don't call him."

The outburst seemed to surprise Mr. Fenstamaker as much as it did Kenny. The big tough bully who relentlessly beat him only moments ago was now reduced to whimpering, crying, and pleading.

Mr. Fenstamaker put his hands on Bobby's shoulders

and sat him back in his seat. "Tell me why I shouldn't call your father."

"It'll just be bad, sir," Bobby said, blubbering and panicked. "I'm really sorry. I'll never do it again. Please don't call my dad."

Kenny watched Mr. Fenstamaker walk over to a large wooden paddle that hung on the wall. He pulled it down, put the handle in his hand, and swung it back and forth like he was checking the weight. Then he walked over to Bobby and held it in front of him, pointing at the surface of it. "Do you see the holes drilled in here, son?"

Bobby, trying to calm himself, nodded.

"Do you know what they're for?"

"To make it hurt more?"

"That's correct. Would you rather I paddle your behind, than call your father?"

Bobby looked up at Mr. Fenstamaker and nodded. "Yes, please."

Mr. Fenstamaker seemed surprised by his answer. He placed the paddle on his desk and put his hands on his hips, staring at Bobby. He looked over at Kenny, pursed his lips deep in thought, and then back at Bobby, who was still trying to stop crying. He took a deep breath and clapped his hands. "Okay, pay attention to me, Mr. Booker."

Bobby closed his mouth tight, but he was still gasping through his nose.

"I'm giving you a mission." Mr. Fenstamaker pointed at Kenny. "You are to be Kenny Pritchard's shadow. It is now your job to make sure that nothing happens to him all year. Do you understand me?"

"What?" Kenny said. He wanted to make sure he heard that wrong. "What are you saying to him?"

"Quiet, Pritchard," Mr. Fenstamaker said, without looking in Kenny's direction.

Bobby looked back and forth between them and shook his head. "But, Mr. Fenstamaker. I can't do that. I can't let the other kids see me with *him* all the time?"

Kenny was thinking along the exact same lines. What would kids think of *him* with Booker hanging around constantly. Now he wouldn't be able to have any friends.

"You have a decision to make," Mr. Fenstamaker said crossing his arms. "Which is more concerning to you, what the other kids will say or what your father will say?"

Bobby looked over at Kenny and chewed on his lower lip. He took a deep breath and pointed at the paddle. "Can't you just spank me real hard with that?"

Mr. Fenstamaker shook his head.

"What if you were to spank me every day for a week?" Bobby asked.

Mr. Fenstamaker held up his hands. "Never mind. I'll just call your father."

"Okay, okay," Bobby said, jumping out of his chair again. "I'll do it. I'll keep him safe."

"I want you to be sure what I'm asking of you here." Mr. Fenstamaker bent down to Booker's eye level. "From this day on, you will make sure that *nobody* picks on him. That he doesn't stumble in the hallway and fall. That he doesn't hurt himself in any way," Mr. Fenstamaker pointed his finger an inch from Bobby's nose. "In fact, if he even stubs his toe, gets a sunburn, or the sniffles, I will paddle you first and *then* call your father."

Bobby's eyes widened at the last part.

"Do we have a deal?"

Bobby looked over at Kenny and crinkled his nose like he just smelled something rotten. He looked back at Mr. Fenstamaker and nodded. "Yes, sir."

Mr. Fenstamaker nodded back and stuck out his hand. "All right then. We have a deal."

Bobby glanced at the big man's hand and put his hand in it and shook.

Mr. Fenstamaker held it firm and made Bobby look him in the eye. "You now have control of your own fate, young man. Do you understand that?"

Bobby nodded again. "Yes, sir."

Mr. Fenstamaker pointed at Kenny. "Okay. Mr. Pritchard is late for class. Make sure he gets there safely."

"Okay, sir," Bobby said. "Yes, sir. Thank you, sir."

He walked out of the room, giving Kenny a glare as he passed. "Come on, Pritchard."

Kenny looked up at Mr. Fenstamaker, hoping the big man would say something like, "Fooled ya!" Or start laughing like it was some sort of joke. But he didn't. He just waved Kenny off with the back of his hand. "Go on, Pritchard. Something tells me you're going to have a great year."

Kenny shook his head, slipped out of the seat, and followed Bobby, certain he was in for the absolute worst year of his life.

Edwards

3

Friday Evening before Thanksgiving

It was nice to be driving the Escalade rather than the Mini Cooper. But as usual, I was running late and I asked Margo if she would be willing to drive herself downtown and meet up with me at the Capital Club for dinner with Casey and Celine. I knew the answer before I asked, because city traffic stresses her out. Her palms get so sweaty, she fears her hands will slide off the steering wheel.

So, I had to drive home to pick her up and then go back into Columbus for the second time that day. Only this time I took US-33. It was a little longer drive, but Margo enjoys the scenery along the river, even in the fading light of the evening.

Margo was regaling me with tales of her day, and how spending so much time with "those women" was almost too much to bear. My attention span for this kind of talk was short, and I found that I was only picking up pieces of her stories here and there.

"And, of course, Ashley Goodman had to comment on it then."

Oh yes, Ashley Goodman. She could be a particular thorn in Margo's side.

"You know she has a comment for everybody and everything, because the perfection bar is set at her life, and if you didn't care to reach that height, then you aren't worth her time."

"Honey, if hanging out with these women is such a horrible experience, then why put yourself through it?"

"Because it's part of being the wife of a CEO. It goes with the territory. And to be honest, I think that we do a lot of good with the charities and our volunteering. I'm very proud of our work; I just don't necessarily like the people I do it with." She looked out at the river, now barely visible with daylight savings time being over. "You don't like everybody you have to work with, do you?"

I thought of Carl Byers and chuckled.

"What?"

"Oh, nothing. It's just that you're right." I waved it off because I knew she wasn't interested in my work problems.

She looked over at me. "Did something happen today at work?"

I nodded. "Something happens nearly every day."

"Well, what happened today?"

"Nothing. Don't worry about it." I didn't want to go into it.

"Why don't you want to share with me?" Here was another one of those moments that, after twenty-seven years of marriage, I have learned how to handle. If I attempt to say that I do like to share with her, but I don't want to talk about it now, the conversation will devolve into how we're not as close as we should be or that I don't respect her views or need her support anymore. Both of which are the absolute *opposite* of true. So, what I've learned over the years is that when that particular sentence is spoken, what she's truly saying is: *You either tell me or we are going to have a conversation that lasts so long and is so uncomfortable that it will eventually break you and then you will tell me anyway, So, why don't you just save us both the time and get it over with.*

"It's just that Carl Byers was waiting in my office when I got there this morning."

"He's on the board of directors, right?"

"Yes. He's the chairman. And he's not too keen on me, to put it lightly."

"What do you mean? What did he say?"

"Basically, he said he didn't like the job I was doing, that he wished I were more like Adam Akers, and that he wants me to resign."

"What?" Margo said, as much a gasp as it was a word.

"Don't worry about it," I said, waving it off, so as not to worry her. It was worry enough for me. "He can't just fire me. He needs a vote of the entire board of directors to do that."

"Can he get it?"

I looked over and saw her face tight with anxiety. I wanted to say, *This is why I don't want to tell you everything. Next time you talk about sharing, remember this and don't push it. There is no sense in both of us worrying.* But instead, I said. "Not a chance. The rest of the board loves me. He just has an ax to grind." All of that was mostly true.

Margo looked back out at the river once more. She was quiet now, which I knew meant she was really worried. I didn't want to stress her more, so I moved on with my day. "On another topic, Isabel's sister dropped by my office today."

Margo looked back. "Emilia? What was she doing there?"

"She applied for a loan to open a restaurant with no experience and no real collateral. When the loan manager told her no, she thought I could go ahead and approve it anyway because I know her."

Margo shook her head. "That must have been a difficult moment for you."

And just like that, Margo reminded me why I love her. She gets me. And this is the reason I'm better off sharing. When Margo shoulders my burdens with me, it feels better than sitting alone and sulking. "It was pretty awful. She is so good in the kitchen that I know she would create a remarkable restaurant. But that doesn't matter on paper, so I couldn't intercede."

"You're right. I get it," Margo said. "That must be why Isabel was in such a horrible mood when I got home."

"*Isabel* was in a bad mood?"

"Oh, yeah. She hardly said a word to either me or the kids all afternoon."

"Wow," was all I could say. I had unwittingly done the impossible. I had put Isabel Alejandro in a bad mood. Now I wasn't even sure if the sun would come up tomorrow. "I wonder why I'm even doing this job sometimes," I blurted out.

Margo looked back at me. "What are you talking about?"

"I mean, who am I helping? What difference am I making? Sometimes I just want to walk away and become a fireman or a paramedic or something. At least then I would know I'm making a difference. Maybe Carl is right. Maybe I should just hand him my letter of resignation."

"And do what, exactly?" Margo said.

I shrugged. "I don't know. I was very happy being a bank manager. I could go back to that."

"Excuse me?" Margo said. "We have built ourselves a CEO's life. Bank managers don't drive Escalades and live in Upper Arlington. Their wives don't go around doing charitable work with other wives. Plus, you have a daughter who is going on her senior trip to France in June, and then she's planning on going to Ohio State next year. What do you expect her to do? Go to community college?"

It was pretty apparent that Margo didn't want me to resign. But I thought I'd string along the conversation anyway.

"First off, bank managers *can* afford Escalades. They may have to buy them used, but they can definitely afford them. Secondly, you were just talking about how irritating it is to be dealing with all of the other wives. It would solve that problem. Third, Amber can skip France, and yes, community college would be great for her. If you'll remember, *I'm* a product of community college. It is not only a top-quality education, it's also a financially responsible decision."

"Ken, you need to think about this carefully." Margo turned in her seat toward me, furrowing her brows. "It's not just what you will be losing for your family, it's what you will be losing for you and your community."

"My community?" I asked. I didn't know where she was going with this.

"Yes. Your disabled community. You've been celebrated as the first disabled CEO of the bank, and you're one of only a small handful of disabled Americans in leadership positions in the entire country. People are watching you, looking up to you. If you just walk away, there could be— no, there *will* be comments about how it was a mistake to hire you because disabled people can't handle it. They already have too much going against them, and so on."

I had to admit it. She was right. There was that angle I hadn't thought about. After several decades, being disabled is just a part of my life. But there are those who were watching to see if I could succeed. I diffused the whole argument by simply saying, "Honey, I'm just venting. I'm not going to quit. Just forget I ever brought it up."

"All right," she said. She sat back and looked quietly out the window while I drove the last few miles into the city.

"Have I ever mentioned the name Bobby Booker to you?" I asked her. I wanted to change the mood before we got to the club, but to be honest there was something nagging me about that phone call all day long.

"Bobby Booker?" she said, letting it ring through her head to see if it sounded familiar. "No. I don't think so. Why?"

"I got a call from Todd Harter at lunchtime letting me know that Bobby's in hospice."

"Oh, that's too bad," Margo said, leaning forward to look up at the tops of the buildings downtown. "Is he an old friend of the two of you?"

"Not an old friend of Todd's. Just me."

Margo leaned back and looked at me. "If he's a friend of yours, how have I never heard the name before?"

"Because I haven't seen him since the fifth grade."

"Oh," she scoffed, then chuckled. "He's not even a friend then. He's just someone from your past."

"Yeah." She was right. Friends are people you try to keep in touch with here and there. But letting someone go for decades and not even thinking about them once—that's not a friend. "Funny thing is though," I said. "Today, I couldn't seem to stop thinking about Bobby."

"No?"

"It's odd, isn't it? After forty-plus years, the news hit me pretty hard."

"I'm sorry, hon," Margo said. And I could tell in her tone she genuinely meant it. My wife was nothing if not extremely empathetic. "Do you think you should go see him before...?"

"I've been considering it. Todd texted me his address. He lives down by Cincinnati." I glanced over at her. "But I don't even know how to do it. Do I just call and say, 'Hi, I'm an old friend from way back and I heard you're on the skids?'"

"I'm not sure I'd use that specific sentence, but yeah. Does he still go by Bobby? The name does seem a little... fifth grade."

I just shrugged and shook my head. Todd called him Bobby on the phone but that was probably so I'd recognize who he was talking about. He probably went by Bob or Robert now.

The Capital Club was inside the DoubleTree Hotel. I parked in the ramp and opened the door for Margo. She stood and gave me one of her beautiful smiles, then kissed me. She looked amazing in her black cocktail dress with lace down the front. She wore a gray cashmere coat with a black faux fur collar. I was always very proud to walk with her in here for dinner.

We were members of the Capital Club long before my current position. I needed someplace to work out, and the local gyms weren't the most accepting places for one-legged men. The Capital Club had incredible equipment and great squash courts.

I opened the door for Margo, and we walked in, passing by the bar where I bought Casey his very first drink when he turned twenty-one and continued into the restaurant.

We were greeted by Eamon, tonight's host. "Hello, Mr. Pritchard. Your son and daughter-in-law are already here."

Margo squeezed my hand. I knew how excited she was about the prospect of a grandchild. I just hoped she wouldn't be let down.

"Follow me," Eamon said. "I'll take you to them."

I truly liked the dining room at the Capital Club. It had floor-to-ceiling windows with a huge view of the Scioto River and the beautiful Romanesque facade of the Center of Science and Industry.

Casey and Celine were sitting at my favorite table, right in the center next to the windows. It used to be hit or miss whether I would get that table until I started at OCB. Now I get it every time I make a reservation. Another perk of being the big guy, I guess.

Casey stood when we entered. He dressed up in a suit for the occasion but already had his coat off and sleeves rolled up. He wasn't really a dress-up kind of guy. He walked over and hugged his mother, and I leaned in and hugged Celine, then we switched.

When all the pleasantries were said, Eamon took Margo's coat and we sat down at the table. He then told us the specials—London broil and pecan-crusted whitefish, took our wine orders, and went off to get our server.

I looked over at Casey. He was gnawing on his third breadstick since we walked in the door and gulping his water. Celine sat there, forcing a smile and staring at Casey. I had a feeling this was not going to be good news. Casey was acting much too nervous.

Margo, on the other hand, was oblivious to the tells. She giggled and jiggled her shoulders excitedly. "So...we have news?"

"Ahhhh, yeah," Casey said. He placed his breadstick on his plate and grabbed his water. Celine just continued to stare at him, a nervous smirk painted on her face.

I was starting to get a real bad feeling about this.

Casey lowered his empty water glass and swallowed with a big exhale. "So, we have two pieces of news actually. The first is..."

"Are we ready to order?" The waiter snuck up on us all while our attention was turned to Casey.

It looked like Margo was about ready to bite his head off, but I interceded just in time. "Give us a few minutes, please. We're having a little family discussion."

"Oh, certainly. My name is Trevor. Just give me a shout when you're ready." He smiled, bowed his head, and scurried away.

I nodded and turned back to Casey, who now had beads of sweat on his forehead. I reached over and put my hand on his wrist. "Son, you look pretty upset. What's going on?"

"I lost my job last week," he blurted out.

"What?" Margo and I said at the same time.

Casey didn't look at us. He stared down at the breadstick

on his plate and nodded. "There just hasn't been the demand for new construction the last few months so they shaved off the dead weight, so to speak." He looked up at his mother. "And I ended up as one of the shavings."

Margo reached out and clutched his hand and spoke in her sweet mothering voice, "Oh, I'm so sorry, honey. It's their loss."

I wanted to point out that they didn't think so or they wouldn't have shaved him out of the business. But that would have gotten me the "not supportive enough" speech so I kept my mouth shut. I also wouldn't talk about how he was vastly over-qualified for that job anyway, having a business degree from Ohio State, but that wouldn't help the situation either. So, instead I tried to get to the heart of the problem. "What do you need from us?"

Casey gestured over to Celine. "We were hoping we could move in with you until I can find something and land back on my feet. Our lease is up, and I can't afford to pay rent now without a job."

"Of course, you can," Margo said, not concerned at all about the "teaching them to fish" concept.

"What is the other news?"

"Huh?" Casey looked back at me.

"You said you had two pieces of news. What's the other news?"

"Oh, yeah." He gestured over to Celine again. "Celine and I are pregnant."

Margo let out a scream that made everyone in the restaurant jump in their seats and scowl at our table. Margo was oblivious though. She was in tears, kissing and hugging Casey, then kissing and hugging Celine, then back to hugging Casey.

I congratulated them both and cheered the good news with our water glasses, making the point of supporting Celine through her pregnancy. When we had all clinked our glasses and set them down, I saw I was getting a look from

Margo. After thirty-two years of marriage, I knew exactly what those eyes were saying to me. With Casey and Celine moving in, there was yet another reason to hang on to my job.

My response was to turn around and raise up my hand. "Hey, Trevor. I think we're ready to order over here."

4

Back in the Day

The next morning Bobby Booker ignored him completely.

Kenny got out of his father's car, walked through a crowd of children by the buses, and saw Booker, Sawyer, Tunney, and Gable standing near the front door of the building.

Other kids pointed at him, some even faked a limp and laughed, but nobody called him names (at least none that he could hear).

Bobby's back was to him when he walked up the sidewalk to the front door. Gable watched him every step and said something under his breath to Bobby, but that was it. There was no incident.

Kenny entered the school to find Mr. Fenstamaker just inside the doors, hands on his hips, watching Bobby and scowling. "Good morning, Mr. Pritchard," he said, without ever taking his eyes off Bobby.

"Good morning, Mr. Fenstamaker," Kenny said, and then walked fast as he could to his classroom before the principal attempted to pull him and Bobby together.

Lunchtime was a different story. Kenny sat at a table by himself, opened his lunchbox, and ate his bologna sandwich with American cheese, and his bag of Fritos. There was even a Twinkie inside for dessert.

Eventually, he was joined by two of his classmates, Maggie, a little dark-haired girl with thick coke-bottle glasses, and Emilio, the only Hispanic student in his class.

"Anyone have anything they want to trade?" Emilio asked.

Kenny shook his head. He'd already eaten everything he had and liked it all. Otherwise, his mom wouldn't have packed it for him. But Maggie was more than happy to trade her oatmeal cookies (which she found dry) for Emilio's Hostess cherry pie.

Kenny noticed Mr. Fenstamaker standing next to the wall, arms crossed in the strange way he did by holding his elbows, looking across the room. Turning in that direction, Kenny saw Booker and the Bookees, sitting together, chattering away and laughing.

Kenny looked back at Mr. Fenstamaker, but Mr. Fenstamaker was no longer standing there. Kenny turned in every direction and saw Mr. Fenstamaker walking behind him and heading straight over to Bobby Booker's table. He walked up, put a hand on Bobby's shoulder, leaned down, and spoke something into his ear. Everybody at the table froze, until the one awkward moment they all looked over at Kenny.

Kenny felt dizzy. He spun back, anxious that Mr. Fenstamaker was going to make Bobby come over and sit with him. His right foot started tapping away, and he looked across the table at Emilio, who glanced up with a surprised look on his face. He threw all his food into his brown paper bag and left the table. Maggie scooped her arm across the table and collected her things into her lunchbox and left right behind him.

Kenny's stomach twisted when one second later, Mr. Fenstamaker escorted Bobby over, hand on his shoulder. Bobby plopped down at the table across from him, looking less than pleased.

"I meant what I said yesterday. You are not to just leave Bobby alone; you are to make sure everyone else leaves him alone as well. You can't do that from the other side of the cafeteria." Mr. Fenstamaker patted Bobby on the shoulder and walked away.

Bobby stared down at his half-eaten peanut butter and jelly sandwich. He glanced to the side to see if Mr. Fenstamaker was still there. When he realized the coast was clear, he muttered, "Don't say one word to me. Got it loser? Otherwise, I'll take care of you outside."

First of all, what Bobby didn't realize was that Kenny had absolutely no desire to talk to him. Secondly, if he "took care" of Kenny outside, he would be kicked out of school. It didn't matter where it happened, Bobby wasn't supposed to let Kenny be hurt. But Kenny did as he was told and remained silent, so as not to poke the bear.

Both boys spent the remainder of the lunch hour in silence. At one point Sawyer, Tunney, and Gable walked by and Gable shouted, "Hey look, it's Bobby and Wobbly!" The three of them laughed and they ran outside. Bobby's face reddened. He took a deep breath and shook his head, chewing slowly while he stared up at the clock.

When the bell sounded to end lunch period, Bobby grabbed his sack and jumped from his seat. "Hope you can make it to class by yourself, *loser.*" And then he ran out of the cafeteria.

Kenny carefully closed his lunchbox, fairly certain he was not going to have much of a lunchtime appetite anymore this year.

When the final school bell rang, all of the kids ran out of their classrooms, down the halls, and out onto the buses to go home.

Kenny limped along the side of the hallway, avoiding the stampede for fear he'd get pushed down and run over. He eventually made his way out the front door and saw his mom's car parked out in the lot. She was the one who picked him up every day. She waved when she saw him, and he headed out toward her car. Just as he was about to reach it, however, he heard a voice from behind him. "Mrs. Pritchard, can I speak to you a moment?"

"Certainly, Mr. Fenstamaker," his mom said. "Is there a problem?"

Mr. Fenstamaker put his hand on Kenny's shoulder. "Kenny, can you go stand by Bobby for a moment while I speak to your mother?"

"What?" Kenny looked back to see Bobby Booker standing on the sidewalk, arms crossed and shifting his weight back and forth. "I don't want to stand over there."

"It will be just a minute, please." Mr. Fenstamaker guided Kenny toward Bobby and then leaned down to speak with his mother.

When Kenny drew nearer, Bobby asked him, "Do you know what's going on?"

"No." Kenny stopped next to Bobby on the sidewalk and turned to watch the conversation.

His mom would look up to the principal and then back at Kenny, nod, and then say something more. Eventually, Mr. Fenstamaker gave her a quick nod and opened the car door for her. She stepped out, walked over to the sidewalk, and held out her hand to Bobby.

"Bobby Booker?"

Bobby looked up at Mr. Fenstamaker, then back at my mother, and shook her hand. "Yes, ma'am?"

"I'm Mrs. Pritchard. I understand you're going to be watching out for my boy this school year."

48

"Wait..." Kenny started, but both his mother and Mr. Fenstamaker put their hand up to silence him.

Bobby looked surprised but managed to get out another, "Yes, ma'am."

"Mr. Fenstamaker tells me you're going to do a great job of it. He says you are up to the task."

Bobby just looked up at her and said, "Yes, ma'am."

His mother smiled, nodded, and said, "Well I want to tell you, I'm very grateful for your help with that. We worry about Kenny since he's been hurt and all."

"Yes, ma'am."

"And I'm grateful you'll be walking him home every day. That will be a big help to me, too."

"What?" Kenny said, but both hands went up again to silence him.

"Yes..." Bobby's head looked down. "...Ma'am."

Now Kenny's mom turned to him. "You have a nice walk home with your new friend and I'll see you in a little bit." Then she spun on her heels and headed back to the car.

"Thank you, Mrs. Pritchard," Mr. Fenstamaker said.

She responded by waving a hand as she walked. She got in her car, backed out of her spot, and drove away.

"You boys better get going," Mr. Fenstamaker said.

Bobby turned and stomped off.

"Bobby." Mr. Fenstamaker called.

Bobby stopped and turned around.

"Wait for Kenny. His mother is counting on you."

After two days of fifth grade, Kenny decided he liked the hospital better. Kenny stormed off too, inasmuch as a one-legged nine-year-old can storm off.

They had walked down the sidewalk about half a block when Bobby threw down his books and screamed, "Pritchard, I hate you!"

Kenny stepped back, but Bobby never came near him. He just fell down, rolled on the ground, and screamed for several minutes. When he was done he sat up, red-faced, breathing hard, and scowled.

"Why?" Kenny asked. "I didn't do anything to you?"

"Because you're a stupid loser!" Bobby screamed. "I didn't like you before you lost your dumb leg because you were such a loser. You've always been a wimp, and you'll always be a loser forever. And now I'm stuck with you the whole stupid year. It's not fair!"

"Listen," Kenny said. "I'll talk to my mom. I'll let her know you're not my friend, you're just a big, dumb, loud-mouthed jerk at school, and I'll have her talk to Mr. Fenstamaker and get us out of this."

Bobby took a couple of deep breaths. "Promise?"

"Promise."

Bobby held up a pinky, and Kenny limped over and pinky-swore.

"Thanks," Bobby said. He rolled over on his knees and stood. Then the two boys headed down the sidewalk together, Bobby taking a few steps, then stopping to let Kenny catch up with him. "Does it hurt?" He asked Kenny after the third stop.

"Yeah, sometimes," Kenny said, limping past him.

Bobby picked up a stick and beat it on the sidewalk in front of him while they walked. After another half block of walking, he starting singing,

"How do you do,

mm-hmm,

I thought, why not,

na-na, na-na

Just me and you,

And then we can

na-na, na-na"

"Why are you singing that?" Kenny asked.

Bobby looked at him like he was crazy. "Because it's only the greatest song in the history of all the songs ever written."

"Oh," Kenny said. "My dad likes the Beatles the best."

"Oh my God, the Beatles," Bobby laughed. "You watch. Mouth and McNeal are going to be way bigger than the Beatles."

"But isn't that their only song?" Kenny asked.

"So far," Bobby said.

"And don't the Beatles have like four thousand songs out?"

"Yeah. Four thousand songs that *stink*."

Kenny didn't say anything more. He didn't need to get into a fight over a song that he actually thought was catchy when he heard it on the radio. Bobby wasn't doing it justice though.

They reached Kenny's house and his mother's car was in the driveway. "She's here. I'll go talk to her."

"Thanks," Bobby said. He stood there a moment, awkwardly and then added, "I guess I'll see ya tomorrow?"

"Yeah, see ya," Kenny added.

Then Bobby continued on down the sidewalk.

When Kenny walked into the house, his mother was standing by the front window. "So, how was the walk?"

"I need to tell you something about Bobby Booker," Kenny said.

His mother waved him into the kitchen. I have some warm cookies and Kool-Aid. Come give me the scoop."

Kenny sat at the kitchen table, happy to see two chocolate chip cookies on a plate with a glass of cherry Kool-Aid, his favorite. He picked up a cookie, took a bite, and chased it down with a drink. The cherry-flavored drink always seemed to go well with chocolate.

"So, what is it you wanted to tell me?"

Kenny set down his cookie and his glass and looked at his mother. "Bobby isn't my friend. He's a big stupid bully at school. Mr. Fenstamaker is just making him act like my bodyguard because he got in trouble for bullying me."

"I know all that," she said.

"Good. So, I need you to talk to Mr...." Kenny stopped,

suddenly realizing what she just said. "You know all that?"

She nodded. "Yes. Mr. Fenstamaker explained what he was making Bobby do, and why."

"Then why didn't you tell him to stop it?"

"Because Mr. Fenstamaker and I agree on something." She reached up and pushed Kenny's bangs to the side. She seemed to like to do that a lot. "We think that once Mr. Bobby Booker gets to know who you really are, he can't help himself but really like you. Then he'll be your *real* friend."

"But I *hate* him," Kenny said, tensing the muscles in his face for emphasis.

"Kenneth Ronald Pritchard, you are not to say you hate anybody."

Kenny knew better than to use that word in front of his mother. "Sorry," he said, sheepishly.

"Just like your principal, I think it's a good idea to go along with this awhile and see how it plays out. If it goes bad, we'll take care of it. But for some reason, I have a good feeling about it." She smiled and tapped his plate. "Now you finish your cookies and relax." Then she stood up to get dinner ready.

Kenny took another bite of his cookie and thought about his conversation with Bobby. Did he pinky swear to get him out of the whole thing, or did he just pinky swear to try?

5

Saturday before Thanksgiving

"Ken, have you heard a word I've said?"

If there was one thing I knew, it was that I was good at getting lost in thought, especially when I'm driving. I was taking Margo to the grocery store to get everything for Thanksgiving, and instinctively when I get behind the wheel, my mind starts racing before I can even put my foot on the gas. "I'm sorry, babe. My head was someplace else."

Margo scoffed, but she was always good about not taking it personally or chastising me about such things. She knew I had a lot going on at work and was supportive. "Okay. We'll just talk when you're not so distracted."

I'm sure she was thinking I was stressed about work, and in truth I was. But it wasn't that or my son's current situation that had captured my mind space. For some reason, I couldn't stop thinking about Bobby Booker. I don't know why. Perhaps it was because the last time I saw him was actually on a Thanksgiving Day nearly 40 years before. Now we were coming up on another Thanksgiving in our old men phase and it would most likely be his last one ever. I couldn't shake that thought. Sometimes you don't concern yourself with someone until there's a chance that they will no longer be there. And then everything about them seems incredibly important.

I pulled into the Kroger parking lot. An older gentleman had just finished loading his car right next to us, so I grabbed his cart and headed into the store. Margo walked along beside me, her hand tucked into the crook of my arm. Oddly enough, I found great pleasure in these simple things. I truly liked doing life with Margo. Mundane tasks such as grocery shopping or raking leaves in the yard were very enjoyable moments when I shared them with her. I wished my brain had worked better the day before when Amber had asked what I was thankful for because I would have told her something silly like grocery shopping with her mom. But these moments were sadly rare ever since my new job. We hired a lawn service and often sent Isabel to the store to do our grocery shopping. I've spent so much time over the years creating a good life, we were now much too busy to live it.

We were crossing over to the front doors of the store when they parted and out walked Ashley Goodman, platinum blond hair and make-up perfect, wearing a plaid wool skirt, knee-high leather boots, and a red jacket with a black fur collar. She was dressed as if she were going to dinner. "Well look at you two, headed in together to buy your groceries for the week," She said. "That is *adorable.*"

"Hi Ashley," Margo said, without any excitement whatsoever.

Ashley held up a bag with two cans in it. "The maid forgot to get the cranberry sauce." She shook her head. "I swear she must have problems reading English or something. Sometimes I wonder why I'm paying her." She chuckled. "Charles will only eat cranberry sauce from the can. It has to go in the serving dish still in that round log shape. I swear, it has to look absolutely fake for him to think it's real." She chuckled again.

Margo smiled to be polite.

After a moment of awkward silence, Ashley gave us a quick wave and walked away. "Have fun in there you two cuties."

"That reminds me," I said to Margo. "I need Ibuprofen. I'm almost out."

Margo chuckled for real this time, then looked concerned. "Really? Already?"

"There's a few left, but I'd like to be safe."

She nodded. "All right."

Once we passed through the Kroger doorway, we went into total hunter/gatherer mode. We were no longer husband and wife, we were warriors on a mission. We both shared the same list through an app on our phones, that Margo had put together, and tackled items on opposite ends of the store, meeting up in the middle. Such as it was when I went to gather all the dairy products, and Margo went off to hunt down candles and napkins with fall leaves printed on them.

As planned, we reconvened at the frozen food aisle and searched for the perfect turkey for our little celebration. I was holding two ten-pound birds when a woman's voice called out, "Ken and Margo! Happy Thanksgiving!" I turned to see Carolyn Wisner, an old friend from college headed toward us with her arms spread wide. She swooped in, kissed Margo on the cheek, and enveloped her with a long, tight hug. Though much shorter, Carolyn stood on her tiptoes and looked over at me with a tight smile. "It's so great to run into you two."

I dropped the two turkeys back into the freezer unit. They sounded like I dropped a couple of bowling balls.

Carolyn released Margo and hugged me. Then she backed off and tapped me on the shoulder.

"You two look like you're doing well." Carolyn was wearing a long winter jacket over a matching sweats outfit. Her hair was cut short and trim, not the shoulder-length do she had back in college.

Margo was smiling. She hung around with Carolyn a lot in college but hadn't seen her since then. "You look great, too. What have you been up to?"

"Well, as you know, when I got out of college I went to work at the United Way. I worked my way up to assistant V.P. of Operations. And I was bit by the nonprofit bug so bad I started my own." She chuckled.

"You started your own nonprofit?" I asked. "What are you doing?"

"It's called 'Study Buddies,' and we help the uneducated and homeless get their high school diplomas, and maybe even an associate degree if they're truly motivated."

"That's amazing," Margo said. "Good for you."

Carolyn nodded. "Thank you. Yes. It's great seeing people who have fallen out of life, for whatever reason, get re-engaged, and so many of them have gotten jobs and started really living again. It's just been incredibly rewarding."

"That's terrific, Carolyn," I said. "Good for you." And of course, the gears started spinning so fast in my head, they were practically blowing my hair around. Could what Carolyn had found as the CEO of a nonprofit be what I was looking for? Would I be happier running a nonprofit than suffering through my CEO job?"

"But what about you?" Carolyn tapped me on the arm with the back of her hand. "Mr. Big Wig Bank Guy."

I smiled at her compliment though right now it sounded like she had the better gig. "Yeah, I got lucky."

"Oh, I don't think so," Carolyn looked over at Margo. "You were always the most driven guy I knew in college. It was just a matter of time."

"Thank you. That's nice of you to say."

"Why are you here?" Margo asked with the excitement of a college girl. "Can we get together?"

Carolyn shook her head. "I would love to, but we're flying out tomorrow. We're just in town to have an early Thanksgiving with my husband's family. I ran over here because they forgot to buy green beans." She put a hand to the side of her mouth and leaned in. "Plus, it was a great excuse to get out of the house, if you know what I mean."

Margo laughed. "Well, I'm so glad we got to see you. Next time you come this way, let us know and give us a chance to connect and meet the lucky guy you married."

"Will do," Carolyn said, and then she proceeded to do the hug-kiss thing one more time before scurrying off.

We finished our shopping with Margo being extremely patient with me. I was so distracted that I started grabbing the wrong items off the shelves, such as cream of celery soup instead of cream of mushroom, which to be honest, I thought could be a nice change of pace because I love celery.

When we made it through the half-mile-long checkout line and were back in the car driving home, Margo smiled and took my hand. "I know exactly what you're thinking."

"You do?" I asked.

She nodded. "You haven't gotten Carol out of your head yet. You're thinking that if you would have become CEO of a nonprofit you'd be making a difference instead of making policy decisions and riding investment waves."

As usual, she had me absolutely pegged. "It doesn't make sense to me. I love the bank. You have no idea how exciting it is to walk in there in the morning, cross the floor and feel the energy of the new day, the new possibilities. When I worked loans, I was setting people up to realize their dreams. It was amazing. But now, I pass through the excitement and walk up to my office. And when Emilia came up, I, being the most powerful man in the bank, couldn't do anything for her. I snuffed out her dream rather than helping her to realize it."

Margo squeezed my hand, smiled, and looked forward. She was wise enough to know when to not say anything. I needed to vent and she let me. She had always been a good listener. So, I felt like I could give her something more to listen to.

"And I also can't get Bobby Booker out of my head."

"Your old classmate who's in hospice?"

I nodded. "For some reason, I just feel I should go see him. We went through a lot together in the short time I got to know him, and I don't think it would be right for me to sit back and let him leave this world without reconnecting one last time."

Margo reached over with her other hand and patted his. "Do what you need to do, honey. But things are getting tight now with Thanksgiving this week so just keep that in mind."

We got home and put away all of the groceries, storing the turkey in a bin in the garage to thaw out. I then exchanged my left leg for a running blade, threw on some sweats, and ran close to four miles. It felt good. I sweat out several pounds along with a lot of stress.

Still when I got back, I didn't have enough courage to pull out my phone and call Bobby—or Bob or whatever he went by now. I took a few moments to start breathing normally again and decided not to be a wimp. I pulled up Todd's text and hit Bobby's number. The phone rang three times before a woman's voice said, "Hello?"

"Ahhh, hi." Todd didn't tell me if Bobby was married or what his wife's name was. "Is this Mrs. Booker?"

"This is Dawn Booker. Can I help you?"

"I'm really sorry to bother you, but I'm a friend of Bobby's...er...Bob's, from back in grade school and I heard he wasn't doing well, so I..."

"Who is this?"

I was messing this up. I could stare down a board of directors, but I stumbled trying to talk to a sick man's wife.

"Oh, I'm sorry, my name is Ken Pritchard, and..."

She gasped deeply, and then there was silence.

"Mrs. Booker?" She didn't say anything. "Is everything all right?" I didn't know if something serious was going on with Bobby. Was it possible that he had died the very moment I called?

Then she spoke, "Is this..." Her voice cracked, and she took a moment to collect herself. "Is this...*the* Kenny Pritchard from Steiner Elementary School?"

Edwards

6

Back in the Day

"So you see, sir. I don't really want him to be around me all the time…or ever, actually."

Since Kenny had struck out with his mother, and she made it clear she wasn't going to talk to the principal, he decided to take matters into his own hands. He got up early, ate his breakfast as quickly as he could, and walked to school, arriving before the buses got there. He walked into Mr. Fenstamaker's office, asked to speak with him, and began explaining how he felt about the situation.

Mr. Fenstamaker sat with his arms on his desk, leaned in, and listened intently as Kenny made his case.

"So, it's fine with me that you tell Bobby he doesn't have to watch me anymore," Kenny said, concluding with a fake smile.

Mr. Fenstamker sat a little taller, pursed his lips, raised his eyebrows, and gave Kenny an encouraging nod.

"I appreciate you coming in here like this and telling me your feelings on the matter, Kenny. It shows a great deal of determination and self-assuredness, and I'm very impressed."

"Okay, great. Ummm..." It was sounding good to Kenny. The principal was saying all the right things, except he left out the most important part. "So...you'll talk to Bobby then?"

"Oh, I'll talk to Bobby," Mr. Fenstamaker said. "And when I do, I'll ask him why he let you walk to school by yourself today."

Kenny felt a chill rush through him. He was suddenly scared that he'd made things worse. "But sir, I just said... and you just said..."

"Yes, Kenny." Mr. Fenstamaker held up a hand to stop him from his meltdown. "I am very happy you came in here this morning to advocate for yourself. It's very important, and you need to do that more often. But it's also important to realize that you won't always get the answer you want to hear."

Mr. Fenstamaker sighed and sat back in his chair. "You will see as you get older that people can be less tolerant of others that are different than them. Take yourself for example. You have already discovered that others are uncomfortable around you because you have an artificial leg and walk with a limp. Am I right?"

Kenny nodded.

"Are you different because you want to be?"

Kenny shook his head.

"Do you think it's fair that you are treated differently than any other child in this school simply because you had a condition that caused your leg to be amputated?"

Again, Kenny shook his head and looked down at his fake leg hanging off the edge of the chair. "No, sir."

"By me telling Bobby he has to protect you helps both of you learn some very important things about one another.

For Bobby, it will teach him that you are no different than any other boy his age. Sure, you have one aspect of you that makes you unique, but you share many of the same interests, likes, and dislikes. This is something Bobby needs to learn."

Kenny looked up, wondering what *he* could possibly be learning out of the situation.

"And what you need to know is that kids your age generally don't act out for no reason at all. There is usually something wrong in their life, and they don't know how to cope. Did you know that Bobby's mother left the family halfway through the school year last year?"

Kenny shook his head.

"I think that Bobby is overwhelmed by life right now and doesn't have a way to release the stress and anger he feels. So, he tends to lash out at others. Worse than that, he lashes out at others who are unable to lash back. In this instance, that person was you. Being your guardian gives him a new purpose, someone else to concern himself with, rather than focusing on his own situation constantly."

"Okaaay," Kenny said, "but with all due respect, what's in it for me?"

"You need to learn to not always make snap judgments about someone who is acting out. People often behave badly because other things are making them angry and have no idea how to cope. It really has nothing to do with you. I think you will understand what I'm saying when you get to know Bobby a little better."

Kenny thought he felt his heart sink into his stomach. The last thing he wanted to do was get to know Bobby any better. He wanted the jerk out of his life.

"So, thank you for coming in this morning." Mr. Fenstamaker said. He tapped his hands on his desk. "And I'll make a deal with you. Since you came in and talked to me this morning, I won't ask Bobby about not walking in to school with you. Sound good?"

"Thank you, sir." Kenny was trying to figure out how he ended up thanking the principal for not doing what he asked. But he hopped out of his chair and hurried to his classroom before Bobby made it to school and realized that Kenny didn't end it like he said he would.

At the start of the lunch hour, Bobby dropped onto the bench across the table from Kenny. He was clutching a greasy brown paper bag and looked at Kenny with an angry glare.

Kenny looked down at his bologna sandwich. "Hi, Bobby."

"Can you explain to me why Mr. Fenstamaker told me to make sure I sit here? You told me this was going to be over today."

"I tried," Kenny pleaded. "I told my mom how horrible you are and she didn't care." He pointed at Mr. Fenstamaker. "I even came in this morning and talked to him and said I didn't want you with me anymore. And he didn't care, either."

Bobby pulled a chicken drumstick out of his greasy paper sack and took a bite out of it. He shook his head and spoke with food in his mouth. "We have to get out of this. I don't want to be stuck with a loser like you the rest of the year."

"I don't want to be stuck with a jerk like you either," Kenny said.

Bobby swallowed his chicken. "Maybe I should just pound you into the dirt and get suspended. That would take care of it."

Kenny was about to agree with him, but then realized that it didn't sound like a workable solution—at least not one that he was okay with. "Won't that get you in trouble with your dad?"

Bobby shrugged. "He's always mad anyway. One more thing won't make that big of a difference."

"Can I have your attention, please?" Mrs. Walters' voice crackled through the speaker system in the ceiling of the cafeteria. "Your principal, Mr. Fenstamaker, has made a slight change to your Friday schedule. He has decided that this year instead of just a Spring Field Day, we will add a Fall Field Day as well."

All of the kids in the cafeteria cheered, clapped, gave thumbs-ups, and high-fived each other.

Bobby and Kenny stared at each other with the wide-eyed realization of what this would mean.

"Be sure to let your parents know and remember to dress for outdoor activities on Friday."

While there was applause, excited hoots and hollers all around them, all Bobby and Kenny could do was continue to look at each other, running the scenarios through their mind. This was going to be a disaster of incredible proportions.

Bobby resigned himself to the tragedy of it all. He threw his chicken leg back into the bag, dragged himself out of his seat, threw his bag away, and trudged out of the cafeteria.

Kenny suddenly felt ill. Perhaps he would start throwing up now. They would have to send him home and if he was lucky, he could be sick until after Labor Day weekend.

Bobby didn't have much to say after school either, which suited Kenny just fine. The buses zoomed by, the smell of diesel exhaust wafting past, making Kenny's stomach feel woozy. Bobby picked up a stick and let it drag behind him.

Kenny looked ahead and saw Sawyer leaning against a fence with his hands in his pockets. Gable, and Tunney standing next to him. When Bobby and Kenny came closer, Sawyer stood, and the three of them blocked the sidewalk.

"Come on, Bobby," Sawyer said. "Let's pound this little snot and get out of here."

"I can't," Bobby said. "I told you. The principal will kick me out of school."

"Then let us do it," Tunney said, taking a step toward Kenny.

Bobby put a hand up in front of Tunney. "Don't even think about it."

"Come on, man." Tunney brushed Bobby's hand aside. "We'll help you." And Tunney started for Kenny.

Bobby dropped his stick, grabbed Tunney by his shirt, and threw him back. Tunney lost his balance and landed on his butt at Sawyer's feet.

"What the heck, butthead!" Sawyer yelled. "That's not cool."

"What's not cool is going after gimpy," Bobby yelled back. "You know what will happen to me if he gets hurt."

"So, you just going to hang out with *him* now?" Gable said.

"We could all hang out together," Bobby said.

Kenny wasn't too keen on that idea. He liked Tunney and Gable even less than he liked Bobby. But he knew he wasn't in any position to open his mouth, so he crossed his fingers and hoped they didn't want anything to do with him.

"Yea, right," Sawyer said, yanking Tunney up from the ground. "No way Booker. You go off and play with your one-legged carrot top, and we'll go find something fun to do."

He walked past Bobby and slammed his shoulder into Kenny as he passed by. Kenny stumbled back a few steps.

"Cut it out, Sawyer," Bobby said.

Gable and Tunney followed Sawyer and looked as if they were also going to slam into Kenny but Bobby pushed them both away. Tunney turned back with his teeth bared and his fists clenched. He glared at Bobby. Bobby took one step toward him, and Tunney ran off after Sawyer and Gable.

Kenny wondered if he had just witnessed the break-up of the Bookees. Only time would tell.

Bobby stood for a moment and watched his friends walk away from him, shouting insults over their shoulders and laughing. Bobby turned, "Come on, loser. Let's get you home." Then he stomped off toward Kenny's house.

7

Sunday before Thanksgiving

I drove through the Colerain neighborhood of Cincinnati searching for Bobby Booker's address. It was a nice, well-kept, peaceful place. Bobby had obviously done well for himself.

It's fair to say I was more than a little surprised when Bobby's wife had recognized my name. And even more surprised that she choked up when I'd called. She told me that Bobby had actually mentioned me and that he even had a picture of the two of us together on the mantle in their home.

It's hard to explain how I felt hearing that. That there was a man who treasured a few months when we were joined at the hip. He was so fond of that time he even kept a commemorative photo on display prominently in his home. Bobby's whole life had apparently been transformed, but I had treated it as completely forgettable. I didn't know if I was feeling guilt or regret.

I pulled into Bobby's driveway, a small brick two-story, with a well-groomed lawn and red and white petunias planted along both sides of the walkway that led from the driveway up to the cement porch at the front door.

I parked right behind a gray van that had the name "Queen City Hospice" on the sides and back. Turning off the car I sat for a minute and gripped the steering wheel. For whatever reason, I was more nervous now than I had been at any time in the past forty years. Margo had offered to come with me for support and I told her that it wasn't necessary. Perhaps it sounds childish, but I really wished she was here now for nothing more than to hold my hand.

I took a deep breath, blew it out through my mouth, then opened the car door and slid out. I walked to the doorway and just as I was about to push the doorbell, the door opened to reveal a short woman with shoulder-length dark hair, glasses, and a Bengals sweatshirt. With a sad smile, she said, "Kenny?"

"Hi. Yes," I said with a nod.

She opened the screen door for me. "It is wonderful to actually meet you. Bobby has told me so much about you."

There it was again, that nagging pain I felt. Bobby had said so much about me, but what was there to tell him? That I hadn't mentioned him to one single person my entire life? My own wife hadn't even heard his name until I got word he was dying.

I stepped through the doorway that opened into the main living room. It was a bright space, painted pastel blue, with a fireplace set along one wall and a flat-screen hung above it. There was a couch facing the fireplace and a La-Z-boy chair off to the side where the hospice nurse was sitting, knitting something. She didn't bother to look up as I entered.

And there, against the far wall, was Bobby, lying unconscious in a hospital bed. Once my eyes locked on him

I couldn't take them off. He was gaunt, pale, and obviously weak.

"You can go see him." Dawn Booker took my coat and instructed me to sit in a kitchen chair that was placed next to the bed facing Bobby. This was obviously her seat that she relinquished to me.

Bobby Booker lie there, no longer the big tough, slightly pudgy, boy he was the last time I saw him. Now he was a grown man, who had seen years of life. Pancreatic cancer had aged him even more. His face and arms were withered. His skin was thin and looked like it was draping his bones due to the muscle loss. There were only a few wisps of hair left on his head, and they still looked like they had never seen a comb. I couldn't take my eyes off him. I stared at him, trying to recognize the boy I knew from the frail man who lay before me.

Dawn leaned over Bobby and shook his shoulder slightly. "Bobby, honey," she said softly. "You have a visitor." She leaned in closer. "It's Kenny. Kenny Pritchard."

Bobby's eyes opened slightly and darted around struggling to find focus. They eventually lowered to fix on me. When there was recognition, they opened a little wider in surprise.

I didn't know what to say at that moment. I suppose something like "Hi Bobby," would have been the normal thing. Instead, I blurted out the first thing that came to my mind and started singing.

"How do you do,
mm-hmm,
I thought, why not,
na-na, na-na"

The surprise in Bobby's eyes softened, and even though it looked like it took effort, the frail face managed to smile. He let out a barely audible, wheezy laugh that caught in his throat and turned into a cough. His chest heaved as he coughed and hacked.

"Okay, okay," Dawn said. She leaned back in and helped him sit up, his skeleton-like hands shaking when they reached for the bed rail for support. He sat and coughed until he dislodged whatever it was that caused him discomfort, and then he laid back and closed his eyes, exhausted from the exertion. His hand dropped, lifeless, from the bed rail.

I looked up at Dawn, horrified at what I had wrought on the poor man. "I'm so sorry."

She smiled at me, tears in her eyes. "Don't be," she said. "I don't think he has laughed or even smiled in weeks. So, thank you for that."

I looked back at Bobby, there was a slight frown on his face now, like he was in some discomfort but was trying to sleep through it. His chest moved up and down from the effort of simple breathing, but it looked like he was trying to recover from a 400-yard dash. I felt horrible. The man was resting peacefully until I showed up and opened my big mouth.

Dawn walked over to the mantle, picked up a small picture frame, walked back, and handed it to me. "Here's one of his prized possessions."

I took the picture and looked at it. There were two bright-eyed youths, little Kenny Pritchard and Bobby Booker, lying in sleeping bags inside the tent that my father had helped us put up in our backyard. They still had curiosity, wonder, and their whole lives ahead of them. It took me right back to that night so many years ago. "This is incredible," I said to her. "He keeps this right there?" I gestured to the mantle.

"Oh, yes," Dawn said with an emphatic nod. "And when people ask who it is, he tells them, 'That's my brother from another mother.'"

I smiled, handed her the photo, and turned back to look at Bobby. This man dying in bed had felt a kinship with me this whole time. I wondered what would have happened had he not been pulled away that Thanksgiving

Day all those years ago. What kinds of friends would we be now? Would we be living near each other? Would we be inseparable? Would we be camping out in campgrounds around the country together, dragging our families along on our adventures, kicking and screaming?"

I handed the photo back to Dawn, who put it back on the mantle.

"Why didn't he ever get in touch with me?" I asked her.

"Oh, he knew you two ran in different circles. But he did like to keep tabs on you," Dawn said, tapping me on the shoulder. "He was so happy when you became the first disabled CEO. I remember him whooping and shaking his fist, telling me and Lila, our daughter, that it was only a matter of time before you made history."

"He said that about me?"

"Oh, yeah."

For a while, neither of us spoke. I sat and watched Bobby struggle to breathe, the only sounds were his rhythmic, wheezy breaths and the occasional click of the hospice nurses knitting needles.

After a few minutes, Dawn broke the silence. "Honestly, I don't think he's going to wake up again for quite a while. I know the coughing jag took a lot out of him and he needs his rest now. Can I get you something to drink?"

I shook my head. "No, thank you. I'll get out of your hair; I should be getting back anyway."

"Oh, you're no trouble, but I understand there's things to do with the holiday this week."

"Yeah," I said.

I stood, leaned over Bobby, and took one last look at the man I shared this unusual connection with. I reached down for his hand and gave it a small squeeze. "Goodbye, best friend," I said, almost whispering, then I turned away, knowing I would probably never lay eyes on him again. "Thank you for letting me come here today," I said to Dawn.

"Are you kidding me?" She wrapped her arms around

me and held on tight. "Thank you so much for being here. I know it meant everything in the world to Bobby to see you."

I hugged her back for several seconds, then we pulled apart and I headed for the door.

"Drive carefully back home," Dawn said.

I stopped in the doorway. "Thank you, I will. It was very nice to meet you."

"It was an honor to meet you," she said and waved to me.

I waved back and headed to my car. I got in, drove out of the driveway and down the road several blocks before I pulled into a church parking lot, put the car in park, and began to cry. For several minutes I cried, without ever knowing the real reason why. I released sadness in my heart that I didn't even know was there. I realized that I had never really cried for the end of our young and brief friendship. I cried now because that friendship could have been more than it was, but I never bothered to give it the chance. I cried because Bobby had built something special from his train wreck of a life and now he was losing it all. I cried for Dawn and Lila.

I cried.

At some point, I looked up and saw two boys, about the same age we were, standing on the sidewalk, holding skateboards, and staring at me. I did what I could to pull myself together. I grabbed fast food napkins from the glovebox, blew my nose, and wiped my eyes. Then I put the car into drive, pulled out of the parking lot, and headed home.

When I had made it to the freeway I said, "Alexa, play Mouth and McNeal, 'How Do You Do.'" Alexa did as instructed and I sang that stupid song at the top of my lungs for Bobby Booker, over and over, all the way home—at one point laughing hard at the fact that now I knew what it was really about. But when you're two kids in fifth grade, the line, "and then we can na na na na," just seemed like lyrical nonsense.

I pulled into the driveway at home to find Casey grabbing boxes out of the back of his Chevy Blazer and heading toward the front door. He smiled and nodded his head to me. I could almost feel my blood pressure rise watching him enter the house.

That's when my phone rang. It was Dawn Booker. I answered and her shaky voice said, "Kenny? I wanted to call and let you know that Bobby passed away a few minutes ago."

It felt like my lungs deflated. "Oh, Dawn. I'm so sorry."

"I just really called to say thank you," she said. "In his last conscious moment on this earth, he laughed. And that gift came from you. So, thank you," She started to cry, but managed to say, "I'll talk to you later." And then she hung up.

I sat in my car staring at the garage door of my home, not knowing what to do, say, or even think.

So, I cried again.

Edwards

8

Back in the Day

Kenny was the only kid in school wearing long pants on Field Day. Everyone else had on shorts and T-shirts emblazoned with Happy Days, Fonzie, Kiss, peace signs, or big yellow smiley faces.

Kenny, on the other hand, was wearing his blue polyester pants that flared madly at the bottoms, and a red and blue rugby shirt with a white collar. He had tried to get out of the day altogether, telling his dad he was feeling sick when he woke up. When his dad didn't believe him, Kenny fought to wear long pants. He felt his limp was enough to make him different from everyone else. He didn't need to wear shorts and displaying his big wooden leg for all of the other students to point at and laugh.

The day was hot, the sun passing in and out of the small puffs of clouds that drifted by overhead. Many of the kids made a game of trying to run fast enough to stay within the boundaries of the shadow underneath.

Steiner Elementary must have looked like there was a student breakout. Every child was outside of the building. All of the kindergarten, first and second graders were together in the side yard having their own field day, and the third through fifth graders were on the back playground where the real competitive games were being held.

Each team had been announced in the classrooms and consisted of nine students—three from each grade. There were numbers along the sides of the building for the teams to meet. Kenny made his way to the number seventeen. Bobby Booker was already there, leaning against the wall with his arms crossed when Kenny arrived. He scowled at Kenny. The other fifth-grade representative was Maggie, with her coke-bottle glasses.

Kenny realized he was the shortest kid on the team. He could have easily been mistaken for a first or second grader, if not for his wooden leg which made him stick out more than anyone else in the whole school.

"Okay, I think that's everybody," said the tall woman standing at the wall by the number seventeen. "Hello kids, I'm Mrs. Bauer, the coach of Team Seventeen. Let's have everybody say their name so we all know who to cheer for."

Mrs. Bauer was a parent volunteer for the day and the mother of Eric, one of the third graders on the team. The other two were Suzie and John, both African Americans. The fourth graders were Juan, who was Hispanic, Ella, a Native American, and Christie who was white.

"It is so good to meet all of you," Mrs. Bauer said.

But Mr. Fenstamaker's voice crackled through a bullhorn. "Okay students, let's settle down and give me your attention for a moment."

It took a few minutes, but the teachers and parent volunteers eventually were able to get their teams under control.

Mr. Fenstamaker stood in the middle of the playground

holding the bullhorn and a clipboard overstuffed with papers. He looked strange to Kenny, wearing blue jeans, sneakers, and a short-sleeved button-down shirt. He looked back and forth at all the teams and waited for silence. Then he put the bullhorn back to his mouth, "Welcome to Fall Field Day. We will be having a series of relays, and team events all through the morning. To allow everything to go smoothly, I need all of you to pay attention, listen to your coaches, and get to where they tell you to be as quickly as possible."

He went through the day's events and talked about scoring.

With each new event he ticked off, Kenny could feel his stomach aching a little more. He looked up at his team members, who were all listening to Mr. Fenstamaker, smiling, most of the kids eager at the chance to compete. The only two people on Kenny's team not smiling were Kenny and Bobby.

The first event was the egg carry relay. All the teams lined up in a long line at the back of the playground. Each student was given a metal spoon from the cafeteria and told not to lose it. The goal was to have each team member carry an egg on the spoon, walk around a cone that was positioned several feet away, hand it off to a teammate who then did the same thing. When all players had completed the run, they were done. Each coach had a dozen eggs to make up for any broken eggs along the way.

When Mr. Fenstamaker shouted "Bang," through his bullhorn, the event began. All along the line, kids headed toward the cones carefully carrying their eggs. The rest of the kids were standing back in the lines, screaming at the top of their lungs. Kenny had been selected to go last.

Bobby had gone first for their team and made it around the cone and back without dropping the egg. He ran to the back of the line and stood behind Kenny. "That's how it's done. Don't screw it up." When each team member crossed the finish line, Bobby leaned into Kenny's ear and said, "Are you paying attention?" or "Don't mess this up for us." John, Maggie, and Christie each dropped one egg, but everyone else managed to make it around the cone and back with little problem and their team was doing fairly well, in fact, so well, they were ahead of the teams that were near them.

Eric was just before Kenny, and he made it around the cone and back faster than anybody Kenny had seen go so far.

"Don't screw this up," Bobby said.

Kenny was shaking by the time Eric slipped the egg from his spoon to Kenny's. Kenny led with his left foot, became off-balanced because of his limp and his egg fell to the ground and broke.

"No problem," Mrs. Bauer said. She ran over and put another egg on his spoon. Two more steps with his pronounced limp and the next egg fell. "Don't worry, Kenny," Mrs. Bauer said. "We have plenty of eggs."

But Kenny couldn't walk steadily enough to keep the egg balanced on the spoon. He was unable to manage more than two steps without dropping the egg. They had lost their lead, and by the time Kenny made it around the cone, he dropped their last egg, and they had to be disqualified.

"You are such a loser!" Bobby screamed at him, red-faced.

"Bobby, stop that," Mrs. Bauer said, angrily.

But Kenny had had enough. This was how the day was going to go, he knew it. He headed to the side of the school and had difficulty finding the sign for Team Seventeen because his tears blurred his vision. When he found his spot, he sat down with his back against the wall, pulled his legs in tight, laid his arms across his knees and buried his head, and cried.

He sat there alone. Nobody came to pat him on the back and tell him it was all right, that it wasn't about winning, it was about teamwork and having fun. Kenny knew all the lines, and he expected to hear them—at least from the coach. But nobody came.

He opened an eye and peered out from the crook of his elbow. Though fuzzy from tears, he could make out Mrs. Bauer talking while the team stood around her, some of them had their hands on their hips, others had their arms crossed and rested their weight on one foot. But Bobby wasn't with them. Kenny looked around and saw an angry Mr. Fenstamaker, clutching Bobby's shoulder and saying something to him. He shook Bobby slightly and leaned in even closer. Bobby shook his head, and Mr. Fenstamaker then pointed at Kenny and said something more.

Kenny buried his face again. After a few moments, he heard footsteps approach. Then Bobby's voice said, "I'm sorry, Pritchard." A moment later he said. "It's okay if we lose."

Kenny raised his head to see Bobby standing in front of him and Mr. Fenstamaker towering behind him, blocking out the sun. "Are you okay, son?" Mr. Fenstamaker said.

Kenny nodded, even though he wasn't. In fact, he knew that nothing about today was going to be okay.

Nudging Bobby off to the side, Mr. Fenstamaker knelt in front of Kenny and put a very large hand on his shoulder. "I can only imagine how difficult this is for you, and you don't need others adding more pressure." He nodded over at Bobby. "Mr. Booker here has generously agreed to be your advocate, your cheerleader today," He turned his head toward Bobby and spoke sternly. "Instead of your critic."

Bobby looked to the ground.

With a pat on Kenny's shoulder, Mr. Fenstamaker said, "All anybody asks of you is that you do your best." He stood in front of the sun again. "And have fun while you're doing it." Then he turned, blew his whistle, and yelled through his bullhorn. "Okay coaches, grab a soccer ball and get your team back to the starting line."

Bobby sat next to Kenny with his back against the wall.

They watched their team head back to the line. Not one of them came over.

"Don't feel bad. They all hate me, too," Bobby said.

Kenny looked over at Bobby, wanting to say, "Not just them. I hate you too." But when he stared at the bully, he saw something different. Bobby sat there, looking out at his team, and Kenny could make out sadness in his eyes.

Bobby glanced over, noticed he was being stared at, and said, "Take a picture, it lasts longer." He shoved Kenny over with his arm, then stood and held out his hand.

Kenny looked up and for a second wondered what Bobby was doing. It took a moment to realize Bobby was going to help him up. Kenny took Bobby's hand and was yanked from the ground to his feet, almost falling forward with the momentum, but Bobby steadied him.

They walked back to their team and stood at the end of the line for the soccer ball relay. Bobby had Kenny stand in front of him. The whistle blew and the event started. They had missed the instructions, but it wasn't difficult to figure it out. Each team member had to kick the soccer ball down the course, around the cone, and then back to the waiting team member.

Their team was doing okay, but the ball got away from both John and Ella and they had to chase it down. Maggie, on the other hand, was surprisingly good at kicking a soccer ball and got the team right back in the thick of the race again. Juan was ahead of Kenny. He took Maggie's kick and headed out with the ball as fast as he could. Kenny stepped up to the line to prepare for his turn. He could feel his team's eyes on him and began to shake. But then Bobby spoke in his ear. "Don't hurry. Go slow."

Kenny looked back and saw Bobby nodding at him. "Just move the ball. Don't worry about going fast and you won't lose it. And if you don't lose the ball, nobody will have anything to scream about."

Kenny looked back to see Juan round the cone, then step

back and kick the ball the remaining distance to Kenny. It sailed high but Bobby caught it and placed it on the ground in front of Kenny. "Go slow!" he yelled.

Kenny shifted his weight to his wooden leg and kicked the ball lightly with his right. It went forward a few feet. He moved to it and kicked it a little harder. It went forward several more feet, but it did not fly off in any other direction.

He heard Bobby scream, "Perfect!" and realized Bobby was right. If he went slow and steady he could do this just fine. He continued his pace of moving to the ball, stopping and kicking it forward a couple yards each time. When he had rounded the cone, he kicked it once more, then positioned himself and gave it one long hard kick toward Bobby. It sailed to the left, but Eric caught it. That was when Kenny saw that the whole team was standing and cheering for him. He had only been listening to Bobby but they were all standing around, shouting, and pumping their fists.

Eric set the ball in front of Bobby who took off from the line like he was shot out of a gun.

Kenny hurried as fast as he could back to the line and John, Eric, and Juan all gave him the Fonzie thumbs-up sign.

Bobby kicked the ball back over the line and Mrs. Bauer put her hand up to signal they had finished. Their team did not win, but they were definitely not last. It felt like a huge victory. They all jumped up and down like they had just won gold at the Munich Olympics.

The teams went into the individual timed events next. Several of them, including Team Seventeen competed in the mummy wrap, where they took turns wrapping one member of their team up like a mummy using toilet paper. Kenny was the obvious choice to be the mummy, not just because he couldn't move as well, but because he was also the shortest and the quickest to wrap up. Team Seventeen won!

Next was a monkey bar relay—a timed event where each individual climbed down one length of the monkey bars, turned at the other end, and climbed back, then they dropped and the next person from the team went.

Only Maggie had difficulty with the event, falling from the bars as soon as she started. She was required to go back to the beginning and start over. When it came to Kenny's turn, he stepped up and launched himself onto the bars. He flung himself down the row, managing to skip every other bar along the way. He swung himself around at the far end and flew back just as fast. He dropped down to the ground and the whistle blew.

When he looked up he noticed that all of his teammates were not cheering for him, they were staring at him with wide eyes and open mouths.

"What was *that?*" Bobby said.

Trying to catch his breath Kenny shrugged. "I don't know. I use my arms a lot to move around when I don't have my leg on. I guess I'm pretty good at arm things."

His teammates laughed, cheered, and patted him on the back.

Kenny teamed up with Bobby for the three-legged race. They tied his prosthetic leg to Bobby's right leg.

Bobby put his arm around Kenny's waist and pulled him in tight. "Lift your other leg and hold on tight," He whispered. "Don't try to run. Let me do this."

Kenny grabbed hold of Bobby's arm, and when the whistle blew he lifted his leg. Bobby ran out ahead of the crowd carrying Kenny on his hip. They crossed the finish line way ahead of everyone else and were immediately disqualified by the judge who was one of the fifth-grade teachers. Bobby untied their legs and then ran over to plead their case but it was to no avail. He turned back and looked at Kenny and both boys couldn't help but laugh.

Kenny happened to glance over at Mr. Fenstamaker. He had his arms crossed and was looking their way with a smile on his face. He turned away and shook his head with a chuckle.

Another timed event had the team throwing a hundred

plastic balls through a small hole in a piece of plywood. They were each given a basket of balls and all aiming at the same hole. Kenny made the shot on at least four out of five throws. Only John was as accurate.

Finally, Bobby yelled, "Give all the balls to Kenny and John."

All of the baskets were set in front of the two boys who made quick work of the task. When John tossed the last ball through, they turned to each other and high-fived. The others members of their team joined in the celebration.

When it came to the last event, there was a three-way tie for first place between teams Eight, Fifteen, and Seventeen. All they needed was a win in the last event—the wheelbarrow race, to seal the victory. Both Bobby and Juan ran over to Kenny to be their teammate in the race.

"No, Booker," Juan said. "I can run faster than you."

"I'm supposed to be watching out for him," Bobby shot back.

The two boys looked at each other angrily and Mrs. Bauer put her hand in between them. "Easy boys. Let's let Kenny make the choice."

Everyone turned to Kenny and waited expectantly for his answer. This was all new ground for him. He had never had anyone fighting over him before for a competition of any sort. He looked up at both boys and knew the choice was clear. Only one of them came over to him after the first event (even though he was forced to by the principal). "Booker is my partner," Kenny said quietly.

"Yes!" Bobby shouted.

Juan bared his teeth and walked away.

All of the pairs lined up along the length of one side of the playground. They had to wheelbarrow as fast as they could across the whole playground, and the pair that reached the other side first won the race for their team.

"On your mark," Mr. Fenstamaker said through his bullhorn.

Kenny dropped to the ground and got on all fours.

"Get set."

Bobby grabbed Kenny's legs and lifted them up. "Is this going to hurt?"

"Not too much," Kenny said.

"I'll let you set the speed," Bobby said.

"Go!"

All the coaches were shouting for their teams, but to Kenny, none of them sounded as loud as Mrs. Bauer. He moved his arms as fast as he possibly could; at times it felt like Bobby was struggling to keep up.

The pair on the right, from Team Eight, worked their way over toward Kenny and Bobby. Kenny glanced over and saw it was Sawyer pushing Tunney. They were doing their best to be a nuisance and for a moment it appeared as if they were trying to crash into them. But Kenny adjusted course and sped up as much as he could, and Bobby gave Sawyer a little hip check, slowing them down. They quickly outdistanced the two, and Kenny realized there were no other teams on either side of them. They zoomed by an orange rubber cone and a whistle blew.

Bobby started shouting. "Yes! Yes! Yes!" He dropped Kenny's legs, grabbed him under the armpits, lifted him like a doll, and stood him on the ground. Then he ducked his head between Kenny's legs and hoisted him up on his shoulders. Bobby started marching around the field screaming and holding his finger in the air.

Soon the rest of the team joined them and jumped up and down cheering.

Kenny had never won anything. He never expected to have a victory like this, especially in an athletic competition. He realized that the best day of his life would not have happened without the help of the big bully, Bobby Booker. He looked around at his happy teammates, trying to soak in all of the feelings so that he would never forget this moment as long as he lived.

9

Monday Morning before Thanksgiving

I walked through the bank on Monday morning feeling a little more buoyant than I had in a while. It was like I had been released from something. I guess crying a lot will do that to you.

After hearing that Bobby Booker had passed away, I cried a whole lot more. I hid away from the rest of the family and our now crowded house, and spent time just with Margo, releasing—emptying—that bucket that I didn't even know was full.

And this morning, I felt lighter somehow. I spent some time thinking about the great moments that Bobby and I shared together—things like our legendary win on that Field Day so many years ago, and I couldn't help but smile.

I waved and said hi to the bank employees by name; "Good morning, Eileen," "Hello Maria," "Hey there, Mr. Paxton. Change some lives today." They all waved, but they were so taken off guard that not a single one of them said anything back. I found that amusing for some reason.

When I stepped off the elevator on the tenth floor, Dianne, pointed to my office. "President Reed is waiting for you."

The Browns had beaten the Bengals the day before, so I knew I'd be hearing from Ryan. I didn't know I'd get the chance to congratulate him personally though.

I walked into my office to see him standing in the same spot where Carl Byers had stood on Friday—he was even looking out the window with his hands in his pockets, just like Carl.

"Hey there, Ryan," I said. "Go Browns."

Ryan turned and I could see he was very worried about something; he looked ashen and almost sick.

"Not just dropping by to say hi, I see."

"I'm afraid not," Ryan said.

I dropped my laptop case on my desk, took off my coat, and gestured Ryan over to the meeting table.

He pulled out a chair, and slowly sat down. He placed his elbows on the table, looking as if he was shouldering the weight of the world.

I took a seat across from him. "How can I help?"

"Well first let me say I'm sorry for putting you in this situation."

I sat back and crossed my arms. "Okay, Ryan. Lay it out for me. Exactly what situation are we talking about here?" I could tell by the look on his face and the fact that he had yet been unable to look me in the eye that this was going to be bad.

He took a deep breath, looked back out the window, and spoke. "The last few years when we've gone to investment group meetings in New York, I've been..." He clasped his hands in front of him and looked down at them. "Seeing someone."

"Seeing someone," I repeated what he said, and he

nodded. It took me a moment to realize what he meant. Then I shook my head. I was disappointed in him and I couldn't hide it. "Oh, come on, Ryan. Are you serious?"

He nodded. "I know. It's awful, and I'm sorry."

I shrugged my shoulders. "You don't have to be as sorry to me as much as you do to Kate."

"Kate's leaving me." His voice cracked.

"I'm sorry," I said. And let it hang there a moment. "I just don't know what it has to do with me."

"Well, they're going to say I promised them things for their silence...." He let the sentence linger.

"They? You said you were seeing *someone*."

"Well, one each time."

"So, how many are we talking about?"

"So far, three are planning to come forward."

"Three?" I took a deep breath and tried to contain my anger. Yelling at him would not solve anything right now. "Well, what did you promise them?"

"What they will say I promised them are insider investing tips, job opportunities, and other...enticements."

"And did you promise these things?"

"Our answer is an absolute no. We're denying everything."

"By 'we,' you mean you and Kate?"

He looked me in the eye for the first time. "No. I mean OCB. We have to deny this."

"Wait," I put up my hands now, just realizing that he was under the impression that I would put up the financial might of the bank to back his infidelities. "OCB can't be a part of this. In fact, I think it's in the best interest of the bank that you step back from your duties until this is settled."

"But Ken," he sounded desperate. "I need you with me on this. I can't lose my job, too. I can't lose *everything*."

Dianne poked her head in the open door. "Mr. Pritchard?"

I looked up at her, happy for the interruption. "What's

87

up?"

"Sorry to intrude, but you asked me to tell you if I heard anything about interest rates."

"Yeah? What did you hear?" I needed some good news right now.

"I got a guy who's an intern at the FTC who said he heard talk about lowering interest rates sometime in the next few weeks."

"Ugh." I shook my head and told her thank you at the same time. That couldn't have been worse news.

"I'm sorry," she said and pointed at the door. "Do you want this closed?"

"Yes, please."

She stepped out and gently pulled the door closed.

"What was that all about?" Ryan asked.

"Carl Byers was in here Friday asking me to resign because he doesn't like the way I run things."

"Byers doesn't like the way the coffee is brewed in the board room. He complains about everything. What does that have to do with interest rates?"

"I bluffed him that I'd heard that interest rates were going to rise to get him off my back. So, this is bad news."

"Ken, you need me. I can fight for you like I've always fought for you in the past." Ryan was angling, but it wasn't going to work.

I shook my head. "Ryan, you have gone and made yourself a liability to me. Your unethical dalliances will just help Byers' argument that I don't make good choices."

"Ken, you can't hang me out to dry." He was almost in tears.

"I don't have a choice," I tried to feel sorry for him, but all I could think about was my daughter, Amber. If someone lied to her just to get their way, I'm pretty sure I would have flown into a rage by now. "Look Ryan, you can't put this on me. These were *your* choices. You can't expect the bank's image to get tarnished because of them, and you can't expect me to let you take me down with you."

Ryan jumped from his chair. "I can't believe this! I have been your biggest advocate ever since you got this position. *Me.*" He beat on his chest with his fist. "I stood on every soapbox I could find to let the world know that even though you were disabled, you were the man for the job. You could handle the pressure, and you were man enough to make the tough calls."

All I could say was, "And this is the toughest call I expect I'll ever have to make."

Ryan narrowed his eyes and pointed his finger at me. He was about to say something but instead just stood in that position. Then he snarled and stormed out of the room, slamming the door behind him. Monday was picking up right where Friday left off.

I sighed, strode back over to my desk, opened my laptop case, and grabbed my Ibuprofen. After taking two of the little lifesavers, I put the bottle back into my briefcase and pulled out the new addition to my office.

I had spent a good deal of time on Sunday night, going through stacks of pictures until I found it—my own copy of Bobby Booker and me sitting in the tent in our backyard. My mother had given one to each of us. I turned and set it on the credenza behind my desk. I had also found the blue ribbon we won on Field Day and taped it to the corner of the frame. I sat back and smiled at the simpler time, finding it funny that I couldn't wait to grow up so that everything would finally be easier when I was an adult.

I turned back, grabbed the TV remote, and turned on the news. I was hoping to see that a sinkhole in downtown Columbus was going to swallow the OCB building immediately.

Edwards

10

Back in the Day

"How do you do, mm-hmm, I thought, why not, na-na, na-na,"

Kenny and Bobby were singing at the top of their lungs while they walked home.

"Just me and you, And then we can, na-na, na-na,"

They were also wearing their Field Day blue ribbons awarded to every member of the winning team. The two boys were happy, and they were letting the neighborhood know it.

"Hey, that's what I'm living for,"

"Oh, my God," came an angry voice from the hedge. "Would you just shut up with that *stupid* song already?" Sawyer stepped out from behind the hedge. "I can't stand that damn song."

Kenny and Bobby stopped. Kenny heard more rustling in the hedge and turned to see Tunney and Gable step out behind them.

"Out of the way, bonehead," Bobby said. "This is the winner's sidewalk."

"Then why are you two losers on it?" Sawyer said.

The other two laughed at the stupid joke.

"Don't be a poor sport, Sawyer," Bobby said. "Just leave us alone."

"Come on, Booker," Sawyer said. "You can't actually like hanging around with this wooden-legged, freak."

"Yeah, Booker. Come on." Gable said.

"He can't help that he has a wooden leg," Bobby said. "But you can stop being a butt plug. It's just your choice not to."

"Fine, then. Move off the sidewalk and we'll leave," Sawyer said.

Bobby took a step forward and crossed his arms. "Make me."

"I don't make pigs like you, I eat them for breakfast." Sawyer shoved Bobby and made him stumble back several steps. Then he turned and ran. Bobby regained his balance and ran after him.

Kenny watched Bobby leave and realized instantly that was a bad idea. He was shoved in the back and fell forward on the hard cement. He tried to turn over, but Gable jumped on his back and started hitting his head. Tunney grabbed at his prosthetic leg and yanked on it. With Gable weighting Kenny down he felt it start to slide off. Kenny screamed for Bobby while trying to cover his head.

A moment later Gable hopped off of his back and Tunney dropped his leg. Kenny rolled over and sat up to check on his prosthetic and saw Tunney ball up his fist. It connected with Kenny's left eye and he fell backward and bumped his head on the sidewalk. Then Tunney grabbed his blue ribbon and tore it off his chest, leaving a big hole in his shirt.

"No!" Bobby screamed and ran past Kenny. He didn't go far this time, coming back quickly so as not to leave

Kenny unprotected.

Kenny could hear the far-off laughter of Tunney and Gable. Then he heard Sawyer yell, "See ya later, suckers!"

"Tell me you're not hurt." Bobby dropped to his knees on the sidewalk next to Kenny and helped lift him up.

Kenny had his hand over his eye and was using all his might just to hold back his tears.

Bobby reached up and pulled Kenny's hand down to see the swelling and discoloration already starting. "Oh my God, oh my God." He reached up and pulled his own hair in frustration. "Can't you ever fight back? Can't you stick up for yourself just *once*?"

That did it. Kenny started to cry. "I'm sorry. I couldn't help it. And you weren't supposed to leave me alone."

"Okay, okay," Bobby said, quietly. "Keep it down. I'm sorry." He pulled his knees out from under him and sank into a crossed-legged position, slumped shoulders, and drooped his head. "This is going to be bad."

Kenny stuck his hand up his shirt and let his fingers stick out the hole. "They stole my blue ribbon."

"What?" Bobby sat up straighter. "Those pieces of...." He stopped himself before he said a bad word. Then he unpinned his own blue ribbon and handed it to Kenny. "Here. You deserve this more than me. We wouldn't have won without you."

"But what about you?"

"Don't worry about me." He shook the ribbon in Kenny's face. "Here!"

Kenny took the ribbon and Bobby jumped up from the sidewalk. "C'mon. Let's get you home so your mom can put ice on your face."

Edwards

11

Monday Evening before Thanksgiving

If there's one hard lesson I've learned in this life, it's to never underestimate the ability others have to really let you down. Ryan Reed's infidelities were more than just a betrayal to his wife and their relationship, they were a betrayal to me, the women he seduced, and the whole OCB institution as well.

Ryan and I had gone back a long time, rising through the ranks together. When it was clear I was rising faster than him, I made sure to bring him along. I knew he was one of the brightest stars in the financial constellation; he just had personality issues. I was one of the few people who understood him. The other one was Kate. As it turned out, neither of us really did.

During the next few hours, I had to deal with the firestorm of Ryan's alleged affairs. It was draining, to put it mildly. I was first on the phone with our public affairs people trying to craft the right statement. It had to say that we don't condone such behavior but that all people are innocent until proven guilty. I told them that he as much as confessed in my office, and I didn't care what we said, but they wanted to make sure he couldn't sue the bank for defamation of character. We had to tow the Switzerland line.

I pulled out of the ramp an hour later than usual and dialed Margo.

"Hi baby," she said, in that sweet caring voice of hers.

"That is the nicest thing I've heard all day."

"I'm sorry you had to deal with that," she said. "That must have been hard. Are you still going to see your father?"

"Oh, crap." I had completely forgotten that I had called my dad the previous night and told him I'd stop by and see him after work. I wanted to tell him about going to see Bobby Booker. I was exhausted but I didn't want to disappoint him. He looks forward to my visits. I sighed and said. "Yes. I told him I'd come, I better go."

"You're a good son," Margo said. "I'll make sure there's a dinner plate waiting for you when you get home."

The Discovery City Residence Home was situated nicely between downtown Columbus and Upper Arlington. It's not like it was much out of my way to see my dad. In fact, every time I pulled into the parking lot I always felt like I should stop by more often.

Just when I put the car in park, my phone rang. I recognized the number. It was Dawn Booker. "Hello, Dawn. How are you holding up?"

"Hi, Kenny. I guess as good as anybody could be under the circumstances. Thank you for asking."

"Sure." I never bothered to tell her that I hadn't been called Kenny since the end of sixth grade. Considering all that she was going through, I didn't think it was necessary.

"Ummm...I was calling to tell you that Bobby's funeral is going to be Wednesday night."

"Wow. That soon."

"Yes. Bobby actually had everything all set for us beforehand. The only thing he said he couldn't nail down definitively was the date." She tried to chuckle but it sounded too sad to be sincere. "Anyway, I wanted to see if you could be there."

I knew that would be a non-starter for Margo. I wouldn't even know how I would tell her that I would be heading to Cincinnati the day before Thanksgiving. "Oh, ahh…" Apparently, I didn't know how to phrase that in a sentence. But I really didn't have time to anyway. Dawn cut me off.

"It would mean everything to Bobby to know you were there," she said. "And I know that there will be a lot of people there who really want to meet you."

"Meet *me*?" I couldn't imagine who it could be or… "Why do they want to meet me?"

"Just from what Bobby has said about you." She took a deep breath, then added, "Please be there?"

I heard myself say, "Text me the information and I'll do my best."

"Oh, thank you. I'll text it right now. See you Wednesday, Kenny." Then she hung up.

I looked at my phone to make sure the call was dead before I said. "It's Ken." Then I slipped it into my coat pocket, got out of the car, and walked into the residence home running over in my mind exactly how the conversation with Margo was going to go.

Once inside I headed straight to the Common Room. It was late enough that I knew dinner would be over and my dad would be watching TV with his friends. When I walked through the door I spotted him immediately. He was sitting with his back to the far wall, so he could keep one eye on the door. He was definitely looking forward to my visit.

He waved at me, grabbed his cane, and struggled his way off the couch. It took him three tries but I knew if I walked over and offered him help, he would just wave it off, so I kept my position by the door and waited. He finally made it to the standing position and caught his breath before heading my way.

I think the greatest disillusionment that we have when we get older is realizing that our fathers won't be all-powerful forever. It's literally the adult version of learning there is no Santa. Watching your dad struggle to walk is the hardest thing in the world, especially when he was the one who carried you on *his* back through your formative years.

But what is even more horrifying to me was watching what happened next. As my father was winding his way out of the TV viewing area, his foot caught on the leg of a woman's walker. He fell forward, his cane flying out of his hands, his arms reaching out to break his fall, but not quickly enough. His face smashed on the tile with a sickening thud, and his head bounced up a little before coming to a full, silent rest.

People say all the time it looked like it was in slow motion, but I think that's because, when something shocking is happening right before their eyes, the mind's camera runs at ten times the speed. Thus, the playback is agonizingly slow. I can still see every split second of it in all its horrible detail.

By the time I got to him, blood was streaming from his nose and mouth. I screamed for him to say something to me, but he was out cold. I called his name a few more times, but the very next second, two nurses pushed me out of the way to check his vitals. I sat back and watched, terrified. I slowly got to my feet and stepped back to let them work. I must have gone pale or something because another nurse asked me if I was all right. Seeing that I clearly was not, he moved a chair behind me and ordered me to sit down. Perhaps he thought I was in shock and going to pass out.

It seemed like one minute later paramedics were rolling a cot into the room. They lowered it all the way and lifted my father onto it. He was still unconscious by the time they wheeled him past me.

One of the nurses brought me a glass of water and asked if there was anyone they could call to come pick me up.

I drank the water, thanked them, asked them where my father was going, and headed back out to my car. I felt like I was looking at the world through those crazy 3-D goggles because I suddenly felt sick to my stomach. I got to my car and steadied myself. I bent way over ready to puke and not get it on my shoes.

When I realized nothing was coming, I leaned my back against the car and called the only person in the world who I could talk to.

"Hi, babe. What's up?" Margo said.

"Dad fell. I saw it."

"What?"

"He's on his way to Riverside Methodist. I'm going there."

"I'll meet you," and Margo hung up before I told her she didn't need to bother.

I was glad I didn't get to say it because the truth was I needed her there. After seeing my dad fall, I needed her to tell me everything was going to be okay.

I took another few calming breaths before climbing into my car and driving away.

12

Back in the Day

"Mr. Pritchard," Mr. Fenstamaker put a hand out and stopped him in the hallway. "What happened to your eye?"

Kenny didn't even try to hide the black eye that Tunney had given him. "I fell down our basement stairs," he said.

Mr. Fenstamaker looked around. Kenny knew he was searching for Bobby.

"Bobby wasn't even near me when it happened." At least that part wasn't an entire lie.

"Where is he now?"

"My dad drove me in today. He was leaving early so I rode with him." That too was not a lie. Kenny had just left out the part where his dad got really mad that he'd gotten hit by another kid on the way home from school, and he blamed it on that "Booker kid."

Just then Bobby Booker walked in the front door and stopped next to Kenny.

"And just what happened to *your* eyes?" Mr. Fenstamaker said.

Kenny looked over and saw that Bobby had two black eyes and scratches on his face and arms. Then he noticed a blue ribbon pinned to Bobby's shirt.

"I got in a fight," Bobby said. "In fact, I got in three fights," he said, holding up three fingers. "And I won them all." He looked over at Kenny and smiled.

"Hmmm," Mr. Fenstamaker crossed his arms and stared down at the two boys. Bobby looked back with a big grin, and Kenny looked up with an expression that said he had just lied and was afraid to get caught. Which he did...and was.

Finally, Mr. Fenstamaker waved them on and walked away. "Okay boys, Get to your classrooms."

At lunchtime, Kenny saw both Gable and Tunney sporting their own black eyes, and it didn't look like Sawyer was even in school that day. When he asked Bobby where Sawyer was, Bobby shrugged and said, "Not my day to watch him."

Kenny and Bobby had discovered a kinship after Field Day. They spent a great deal of time together. Even on weekends, Bobby would come down to Kenny's house to play. But Bobby never let Kenny come to his house, saying it wasn't really fun there anyway. They played catch in the backyard, tried to catch minnows and polliwogs in a creek a few blocks away, and spent hours playing Pong on the basement TV (much to the dismay of Kenny's mom, who thought they should be outside getting fresh air).

At one point Bobby wanted to teach Kenny how to ride a bike so they could ride to the movie theater on Saturdays. Kenny explained how his father had tried to teach him but when couldn't keep his left foot on the pedal, he'd stopped trying.

Kenny was eating breakfast one day and the doorbell rang. His mother answered it to find Bobby holding up a gigantic rubber band. "Hi, Mrs. Pritchard. This will help Kenny ride a bike. Can he come out so we can try it?"

Bobby strapped Kenny's left foot to the pedal and Kenny's father held him up while he tried to ride. It wasn't long that Kenny realized his foot wasn't going to fall off and he could stay upright without his father's help. He started pedaling faster and soon outdistanced his dad and Bobby. They stood back and cheered for him. When Kenny turned around he saw them high-fiving each other.

Riding a bike opened up the world for Kenny. He could now go farther distances without having to worry about getting too tired to make it back home. The rubber band that Bobby had used as a strap snapped after just a few days of use, but Kenny's dad rigged up a small bungee cord to the pedal which made it easy for Kenny to slip his foot in and out with relative ease.

Feeling like a ride on a very warm Saturday morning in October, Kenny hopped on his bike and rode to Bobby's house to see if he wanted to go into town. He parked in the driveway. The garage door was open, and a big rusty Ford truck was in the garage. He noticed Bobby's lawn was longer than the rest of the lawns in the neighborhood and was filled with all the weeds that his own father always worked so hard to kill off. When Kenny walked toward the door, he noticed a thick layer of grime on the windows that his own mother always washed off every spring. He could almost smell the vinegar just thinking about it.

The front door was open to let in fresh air. He heard a gruff man's voice through the screen. "Look at that. You think that bowl is clean?"

Kenny stopped before he reached the porch. He heard Bobby's voice say, "Sorry, Dad. I'll do it again." Bobby sounded nervous and scared, which was strange to Kenny.

"I asked you a question." The man's voice sounded angrier. "Is that clean? I didn't ask you to wash it again. Are you a dummy?"

"No Dad. It's not clean," Bobby said. "I'll wash it again. I'm sorry."

"No you won't, dummy. I'll get it. You're too stupid to get it clean. All I want is to get cereal in a clean bowl in the morning, and my dumb son can't even do that."

"Sorry, Dad."

"Sorry?" The man screamed. "That's all I get from you, 'Sorry Dad, sorry Dad.' You're the sorriest kid I've ever seen. Sorry for your grades, sorry you're always getting in trouble, sorry you're too dumb you can't even clean a bowl right. I'm tired of your sorries. You hear me?"

"Yes, Dad." Bobby sounded pained.

Kenny turned around and hurried back to his bike. He heard a large thump and a crash come from Bobby's house. Then the man screamed once more. "Now get out of this house. I can't even stand to look at you right now, dummy."

Kenny slipped the pedal strap over his left foot and was about to ride away when Bobby came running out the screen door of his house. He was crying, but when he saw Kenny, he rubbed his eyes and pulled himself together.

"What are you doing here?" he asked, his voice had a hard edge.

"I just…" Kenny started to say, but Bobby ran over and hissed at him.

"I told you not to come over here."

"Wanna ride?" Kenny asked.

Bobby glared at him a moment more, but then his expression softened and he nodded. He ran into the garage, grabbed his bike and the two boys pedaled away from the house as fast as they could.

Instead of heading downtown, they headed out to the creek, parked their bikes, and sat on the bank, tossing pinecones into the water and watching the current carry them away.

Kenny gave Bobby a moment to relax before he asked. "Why was your dad so mad?"

Bobby swatted at a mosquito. "He's always mad."

"Because you can't do dishes very well?"

Bobby looked over at him and frowned. "How long were you standing out there?"

Kenny tossed another pinecone and watched it splash in the center of the creek. "Not long?"

"Long enough to hear about the damn bowl."

Kenny nodded. He waited another moment before saying, "I heard him say you were dumb."

Bobby shrugged. "Guess I am."

"No you're not," Kenny said. "You were the one who figured out how to fix my bike so I could ride it."

"That's easy crap," Bobby said. "That's not math. I'm a dummy when it comes to math."

"I can do math," Kenny said.

"You don't have to rub it in."

"No. I'm not bragging. I mean I can help you."

Bobby looked over at him like he was waiting for a punchline. When it didn't come, he said, "You think so?"

"I know so," Kenny said. "Math is about the only thing I'm good at. *I'm* a dummy at everything else."

Bobby laughed.

That evening, when Kenny's mom was tucking him in bed, he brought up what he'd overheard earlier in the day. "Bobby's dad called him a dummy."

"Yeah?" His mom said.

"Yeah. A *lot.* Over and over again."

His mother nodded. "I suspected something like that."

"You did?"

"I did." She sat on the edge of his bed. "You see, some people have very hard lives and they have trouble dealing with it. When they get really frustrated they lash out at the people they love."

"It didn't sound like Bobby's dad loves him."

"He does. He's just not able to show it because he's filled up with too much sadness." His mom leaned in close. "It just means you have to work at being an extra great friend to Bobby, so he knows somebody cares, okay?"

Kenny nodded and she kissed him on the forehead. "Now get some sleep." Then she left the room, turning off the light but leaving the door open just a crack like he liked it.

Kenny looked up at the glow-in-the-dark stars on the ceiling of his room and thought about what she said. He already thought he was an extra great friend. Did she mean he wasn't doing enough? Perhaps helping Bobby with math would be all the extra work he needed to do.

13

Tuesday Morning before Thanksgiving

My head was pounding by the time I reached my parking spot at OCB. My guess it was lack of sleep. I stayed at the hospital with my dad until 2:30 am. He was hurt pretty bad. He had a laceration on his forehead and, worse, a concussion. He wasn't in great shape but good enough to go back to the residence home, and I got him back without too much difficulty. Then I got home and went to bed, except it felt like my head just hit the pillow when the alarm went off. I was exhausted and needed coffee immediately.

I popped two ibuprofen while I was still in the car and then headed into the building.

For only the second time since I'd moved my office downtown, I decided to take the front elevator to the tenth floor. I just couldn't force myself to walk through the bank and say hi to anybody, pretending everything was all right. All I wanted to do was climb into the hole of my office and be alone, leave the world behind.

Dianne looked confused for a moment when she saw me emerge from the hallway rather than the elevator by her desk. "How's your father?"

I was surprised she even knew about him.

"Margo called me."

I nodded. Of course, it was Margo. She was always behind the scenes making sure I was taken care of. "I dropped him off back in his room and he was resting comfortably. But I think he's going to have a headache today as bad as mine is." I started to head into my office but stopped myself and turned back to her. "Thank you for asking."

"Sure thing," she said. "There's a hot cup of coffee waiting for you on your desk."

I looked back, and she knew what I was thinking. I'd made it clear from the first day she came to work that she was *not* to get my coffee. That wasn't what I expected out of an assistant. I was an adult who could get his own coffee, and she had enough to do.

She shrugged and smiled. "Just let someone do something nice for *you* for a change and say 'thank you.'"

I chuckled and did as she ordered. "Thank you." Then I walked into my office, hung up my coat, and sat down, taking a moment to look at the picture of Bobby and me that was sitting on the credenza. I realized that I'd forgotten to tell Margo about Bobby's funeral. It had completely slipped my mind with the drama of the previous night. But I didn't see how I could make it now anyway. Not with everything that happened with my dad and Thanksgiving the very next day. I would just have to call Dawn Booker back and break the news.

I pulled my laptop out of its case, slipped it into the dock, and waited for my monitor to come to life. All I wanted to do was get lost in the mundane tasks of the day when Dianne walked in. "We've had requests from the *New York Times,* the *Wall Street Journal, the Columbus Dispatch,* and NBC

News, all wanting to talk to you."

"Already?" I couldn't believe it. I had just sat down.

Dianne nodded. "They were actually from last night. They left voicemails." Just then her phone rang. "And that's probably someone else trying to get hold of you."

"But we gave a great statement yesterday. I worked all day on it."

"Do you want me to just refer them to that?"

"Yes, please."

She turned to leave.

I pressed at the sides of my temples, praying the ibuprofen would start taking effect soon. Then I heard Dianne say. "Excuse me, he has appointments all morning long and can't be disturbed."

I looked up to see Carl Byers with two other members of the board, Sandy Haggerton, and James Ngo, marching into my office with Dianne on their heels.

"This is the only appointment he needs to concern himself with today," Carl said.

Dianne looked at me and I held up a hand, nodding that it was all right. She walked out and made a point of leaving the door open. I should have realized after the bombshell dropped about Ryan, that I would be hearing from Carl very soon. He had to have his chance to lord it over me that I'd made another bad decision.

My head felt like an arrow had pierced it, but I gathered myself together and said, "What can I do for you?"

"I've brought two more members of the board with me who are now as unhappy with your performance as I am," Carl said, nodding at James and Sandy. "And I guess all you can do for us is tell us when you plan to pack your things."

James crossed his arms. Sandy looked over at him and then back at me. She gave a stiff upper lip and nodded.

"You see I received a very interesting call last night," Carl said. "It was from a disgraced president of this very bank with an ax to grind. He let me know that you lied to me about the Fed raising interest rates."

"What?" There was a sharp pain in the center of my back. Was it my mind's manifestation of Ryan's knife? I couldn't believe that he was capable of selling me out like that. But then why should I have been surprised after what he'd already done in New York.

"Yes. Apparently, your decisions were incredibly poor all the way around." Carl said. "Now, would you like to negotiate a severance deal? Or are we going to go ahead and take this all the way to Monday?"

I struggled to catch a breath and began to wonder if this is what a panic attack felt like. I loosened my tie and unbuttoned the top button of my shirt.

"Cat got your tongue?" Carl said, adding a chuckle at the end of it so it sounded extra snide.

My headache had evolved into a full-blown migraine at this point, and the light was hurting my eyes. I put my hands over them briefly, hoping that would make the throbbing lessen a bit. But when I pulled them away to address the board members in front of me, something had happened. They no longer looked like Byers, Haggerton, and Ngo. It was as if they'd been replaced and the three people now standing in front of me were Sawyer, Gable, and Tunney— simple thugs who had no more purpose in life than to cause me grief.

And then I heard a voice. "Can't you ever fight back?" It was Bobby Booker's fifth-grade voice pounding through my head, prodding me on. "Can't you stick up for yourself just *once*?"

Bobby was right. I did need to stick up for myself. And now that I was bigger than them, I would show them I was no longer afraid of them.

"He doesn't look so good," Tunney said. "Ken, are you all right?"

"He's fine," Sawyer said. "He's out of options, so pretending he's sick is the only way to get us to leave."

I placed my hands on the top of my desk and pushed myself up out of my chair. It must have been a lot of work because I started to sweat. "I think it's time for you guys to go home," I said. "Pigs like you need to be fed by nine a.m."

Sawyer looked confused. "What?"

"No, something's really wrong with him," Gable said.

Just then Dianne ran past them. "Oh my God, Ken. Sit back down!"

I raised a shaky arm and pointed at the three bullies. "Not until..." But that's all I could say because at that moment a pain hit my chest so hard, it knocked the wind out of me. I tried to steady myself on the desk, and that's when the room started spinning and I lost my balance. The floor came up to meet me, and the impact jarred every bone in my body. I struggled to breathe because something was crushing my chest.

In the distance, I heard Dianne scream, "Call 9-1-1!"

And then I drifted away.

Edwards

14

Back in the Day

Bobby was waiting on his bike in the driveway the day Kenny arrived home from the doctor's office after being fitted with his new leg. "Can I see it?" Bobby said.

Kenny turned in his car seat and pulled up his pant leg to reveal the sleek new prosthetic. "It's made of space plastic like NASA uses. It's really hard."

Bobby knocked on it with his knuckles and then looked up at Kenny, "Did that hurt?"

Kenny laughed and shook his head.

His dad walked on into the house. His mom stopped at the front door and looked back. "Dinner's in just a few minutes, Kenny. I have stew in the Crockpot. Do you want to stay for dinner, Bobby?"

Bobby looked up over the car. "No thank you, Mrs. Pritchard. I have to be home for dinner."

She nodded and continued in.

Kenny climbed out of the car. "Watch me walk." He walked up and down the driveway. His new prosthesis was much lighter than his old wooden leg, so he didn't have to drag it along with him. Kenny found that he could walk much easier with only a small limp.

"Oh my God, Kenny," Bobby said with his hands on his head in disbelief. "You're walking almost normal."

"I know," Kenny said. He couldn't stop smiling.

"No, this is great," Bobby said. "I'll bet you could run with that thing."

Kenny stopped walking and stared at Bobby. He hadn't thought about that.

"I saw this thing on TV on Saturday," Bobby said. "It came on right after Scooby-Doo, and it was about the Paralympics."

"Para...?"

"Yes, Paralympics. It's where people from all over the whole world, who've lost legs and arms and stuff, run races and things like that. It's like a real Olympics except it's for people just like you."

"I..." Kenny didn't know what to say. He just got the leg and was trying to get used to walking with it. Running races was a little too far ahead for him right at the moment.

"Hey look," came a shout from across the street. "It's Gimpy and Wimpy!"

Both boys looked to see Sawyer, Gable, and Tunney riding by on their bikes. Tunney laughed. "Gimpy and Wimpy. That's a good one."

"Come 'ere and say that!" Bobby yelled. "I'll show you who's wimpy—again!"

Sawyer flipped his middle finger at Bobby then all three of them sped off.

"Damn jerks," Bobby said.

Kenny's dad came out the front door. "Hey, Kenny." He walked out to the driveway. "Did you talk to Bobby about what we discussed in the car?"

"No, not yet," Kenny said.

"Why don't you do it now, before he goes home so he can ask his dad?"

Bobby walked back. "What is it?"

"Do you want to camp out in a tent in my backyard on Saturday night?" Kenny said.

"You mean all night long?" Bobby sounded excited.

"Yes," Kenny's dad said. "It's supposed to be warm this weekend, and it's probably the last time that will happen for a while. I'll set the tent up in the back yard, and you boys can sleep out there. You can come in to use the bathroom if you need to."

Bobby was so excited he hopped on his bike right then to go ask his dad. Kenny went in and washed his hands, and just as he sat down for supper, the phone rang. His mother answered and it was Bobby letting them know that he could camp out on Saturday.

Mr. Pritchard had a list of things for the boys to do when Saturday had arrived. The first thing was to rake up the bright yellow, orange, and red leaves where they planned to pitch the tent.

Then they had to figure out *how* to pitch the tent. Kenny's dad stood by and talked them through it but was determined that the boys put the tent up themselves. It was the only way they'd learn, he said.

Kenny's mom brought out a hibachi. "Here, you can use this to build a small fire and roast hot dogs and marshmallows," she said. "But you'll have to set it up on cement blocks and gather the wood for the fire."

After setting up the hibachi, the boys fetched a cooler and loaded it with ice for sodas and snacks.

"We put the snacks in the cooler, so the raccoons and rodents can't get at 'em," Kenny explained to Bobby, who was brand new to all this.

Kenny's dad got the fire lit while the boys put their

sleeping bags and pillows in the tent. They also added a radio and ran the extension cord to the house so they could listen to some music.

Finally, the fire was lit and it was time to cook their hot dogs. Kenny's dad gave them each their own sticks to cook with, and Kenny's mom brought out a tray filled with plates, ketchup, mustard, bags of Fritos, and a box of Hostess Ho Hos. Dad filled up the cooler with different flavors of Faygo soda and tied a can opener to the cooler handle with a string so it wouldn't get lost.

When all was set, Kenny's folks went into the house and left the boys to cook and fend for themselves. Bobby gave Kenny both hot dogs to hold while he got up and got their sodas—a Rock and Rye for himself and a Fruit Punch for Kenny.

While they cooked and ate, Kenny tested Bobby on different math problems he could do in his head, and Bobby talked about his plans to get Kenny ready for the Paralympics. "The next one is in Toronto, next year, but you're too little. But in four more years, it will be in Arnhem in the Netherlands. You'll be bigger then and we can go to that one."

It was dark out by the time they had polished off all the hot dogs, and the whole box of Ho Hos. It was time for bed so they went inside and changed into their pajamas and brushed their teeth.

Kenny removed his leg and used his crutches to head out to the tent. Bobby watched with fascination as his empty pajama leg swayed back and forth while he walked.

Once they crawled into their sleeping bags, Kenny's mom was at the door of the tent with the Kodak camera. "I have two pictures left on this roll, let me get a shot for each of you."

They smiled while the camera flash went off twice. "Great job," she said. "I'll drop these off when I get groceries this week and you'll have them, I bet, by Friday."

"Thank you, Mrs. Pritchard."

She zipped up the tent and they laid back, making shadows with their flashlights, and listened to the radio. Bobby waited for his favorite song, but the disc jockey never played it. They talked about their favorite TV shows, Kenny's was *Welcome Back, Kotter* and Bobby's was *Wonder Woman* because Linda Carter was a fox.

When there was silence for a few moments Bobby spoke up, "Can I ask you something?"

"Uh-huh,"

Bobby rolled over and looked at Kenny. "What was it like to lose your leg."

Kenny shrugged. "I don't know. Sad, I guess."

"But didn't it hurt?"

Kenny looked up at him. "I wasn't awake. They took me into an operating room and put me to sleep. When I woke up my leg was gone. But then it *really* hurt."

"Were you scared when they took you in?"

"Yes," Kenny said, taking a moment to think back on that time. "But the nurses were nice, so they helped keep me calm."

Bobby nodded and rolled back over.

"Can I ask *you* something?" Kenny said.

"Yeah."

"You've been different ever since that time at Field Day when Mr. Fenstamaker talked to you. What did he say?"

"He just asked me..." Bobby took a deep breath. "He asked me how I would feel if people made fun of me because my mother left. It was something that happened to me, that was completely out of my control, just like losing your leg was to you. It made me different from everyone else but exactly the same as you because we had both lost something important. He asked me if I would like being called a loser because I had no mother."

Then a voice was heard outside the tent. "You are a loser because your mother left." Followed by laughter from two other boys.

Bobby bolted upright. "Sawyer, get your ass outta here."

Sawyer laughed. "Your mom left because you're so butt ugly she couldn't stand to be seen with you."

Bobby scrambled out of his sleeping bag and unzipped the tent flap. As soon as it opened up, he was hit in the head and chest with three eggs.

Sawyer, Tunney, and Gable sounded like roosters they were laughing so hard. They started to run away, but Bobby caught Gable from behind, pulled him to the ground, and started beating on him. Sawyer came back and tackled Bobby off of Gable.

"Leave him alone!" Kenny screamed, unable to do anything because his leg was in the house.

Suddenly a commanding voice ended all of the commotion. "Stop that, right now!" Kenny's dad burst out of the house.

"Let's go!" Tunney screamed, and the three thugs ran out of the yard as fast as they could.

Mr. Pritchard ran out to Bobby and helped him up. "Are you hurt?"

Bobby was breathing hard and trying with all his might not to cry. Egg yolk and shells dripped from his hair down his face and stuck to his pajamas.

Kenny's mom rushed him into the house and cleaned all of the mess off with a warm washcloth. "You're much bigger than Kenny or I'd give you a pair of his pajamas to wear."

Bobby assured her his pajamas would be fine and they'd dry out soon enough. When he was all cleaned off, he climbed back into the tent, slid into his sleeping bag, rolled over, and said nothing.

"Do you want to talk?" Kenny asked him, but Bobby didn't say another word.

In the silence, Kenny thought about the transformation. Bobby Booker had been the biggest bully in the school until he became Kenny's friend. And now he was just another kid being bullied, feeling just as bad as Kenny always did. After a few more minutes Kenny rolled over, too. He was all worked up from the excitement of the evening but sleep finally overtook him.

Edwards

15

Tuesday Evening before Thanksgiving

Another day, another visit to the ER.

Margo would not let go of my hand at any point while we were in the room together, though she was forced to release me when I was sent off to every test ever invented. I had the entire round, from an EKG to an X-Ray, to an MRI, to an ECG, all approved by the FDA, the CDC, and the DOJ. I think there were one or two others that I couldn't remember the acronyms to because I fell asleep here and there. Now we were just waiting for the battery of test readers to finish their readings so the doctor could come in and tell us what the hell happened.

ESPN was on the TV and there was a debate about who would make it into the college football playoffs. I tried to be interested, but it looked like my beloved Buckeyes were out this year because of one back-breaking loss against Michigan State.

I glanced over at Margo who looked lost in her worry. She stared at my hand—her thumb moving gently back and forth across my knuckles.

I shook the hand to break the spell she was under. "Hey there."

Her head turned slowly up to me. I'd never seen her so worried before in all the time we'd been married.

"You're going to die from worry," I said, hoping my smile would bring her back to the real world. "Stop that. I'm right here and I'm fine."

Her eyes teared up instantly. "You don't know that."

"What?" I chuckled. "I know that I'm here. And I know that I'm alive. And anything else will be taken care of by the fine medical staff at this hospital."

Margo stood, took a step toward the sink, and reached for a couple tissues out of a box, never once letting go of my hand. She sat back down and wiped her eyes. Then she looked back at me. "I've been sitting here and trying to picture my life without you in it, and it's unbearable to even think about."

I shook her hand again. "Don't think about it."

Then she looked determined. "Whatever this is, you have to promise me that you are going to take care of yourself from now on. It's time for you to get healthy."

"What are you talking about?" I am healthy. I'm not overweight—too much, and I run, usually with *you*."

She cocked her head slightly. She always did that when she was about to make a point that was going to sting. "And you have Jimmy John's for lunch *every* day."

Yep. It stung. "This is not because I eat Jimmy John's."

"Seriously, Ken. What man in your position eats Jimmy John's for lunch every single day? Wait. I'll tell you. Not a single one."

"I don't have it *every* day." I pleaded. "Sometimes I'm forced to go to business lunches."

The door opened, and two doctors walked in.

"Mr. Pritchard?" said the older one, an African American with graying hair. He walked up to me with his hand out. I shook it. "I'm Dr. Massey, and I'm a cardiologist." He held out his hand to Margo, and she shook it awkwardly with her left hand, still not willing to let go of my hand with her right.

Dr. Massey nodded toward the other doctor, "And this is Doctor Rahim."

Doctor Rahim stepped forward and offered his hand as well. "Good to meet you both."

Dr. Massey pulled the computer cart over to him and logged in. "So, the results of all of your tests are in, and Doctor Rahim and I have looked at them extensively."

I looked over at Margo. She was staring at Dr. Massey with big fearful eyes. I shook her hand again and she looked over at me. I mouthed the word "relax" which seemed to annoy her more than anything else.

"It appears what happened to you today," Dr. Massey continued, turning his gaze from the monitor to Margo and me. "Is what's known as stress-induced cardiomyopathy."

"Does that mean heart attack?" Margo asked quickly.

"No, and yes," Dr. Massey said. "Yes, because it did result in some damage to the heart,"

Margo's hand squeezed my hand hard. I could tell she wanted to scream.

Dr. Massey continued. "And, no, it's not a heart attack based on the typical reasons, such as a blockage in the arteries. Your arteries and blood flow look fine."

"So, this has nothing to do with eating, say…"
I shrugged. "Jimmy John's sandwiches at lunch for example."

Margo glared at me. "Are you really being serious right now?"

Dr. Massey and Dr. Rahim looked at each other and chuckled.

"Looks like a little debate was going on before we arrived," Dr. Rahim said.

"I think so," Dr. Massey said. He looked back at us. "Well, let me put it this way. This particular incident isn't a result of eating Jimmy John's, but too many of them and the next one could be."

"Thank you, doctor." She gave me a smug look and then turned back toward him.

"This is more the result of severe emotional stress. Would you say you've been dealing with stress, Mr. Pritchard?"

I thought about what had been going on when it hit. Carl Byers and company were coming in to threaten me about my job.

"He's the CEO of a bank," Margo said. "He has a very stressful job."

"I see." Dr. Massey slid the stool over and sat next to me. "Well, this is something that will need to be figured out. There are multiple things you can do to manage stress, and you have to. Stress can lead to a variety of issues." He gestured toward my heart. "The damage that has occurred here is reversible but this is a very serious warning sign that stress is affecting your health. And if you do nothing, the stress can lead to much more serious problems such as heart disease, diabetes...even Alzheimer's disease."

"What can we do?"

"I'll get you some materials on things you can do to reduce and manage your daily stress," Dr. Rahim said. "But you have to realize it is going to require a lifestyle change."

"Yes," Dr. Massey said. "With you having such an important and demanding job, you're going to have to be very vigilant with it all."

"Okay. Thank you," I said while wondering how to go about managing stress when it was my job to manage all of the stressful situations at OCB, not to mention my own issues. "So, what's next for me right now?" I said.

Dr. Massey stood and slid his stool back off to the corner. "I want to get you admitted so we can keep an eye on you tonight. I will stop by in the morning and see how you did. If everything looks good, we can get you out of here."

The doctors shook both our hands again and left the room.

Margo stood and looked over me, still clutching my hand tight. "I'll do whatever it takes to help you out, babe. You just tell me what you need and you'll have it."

I don't know why certain thoughts hit you when they do, but for some reason, a specific thing fired into my brain just at that moment and I didn't hesitate to say it. "I need to go to Bobby Booker's funeral tomorrow."

Edwards

16

Back in the Day

The morning following the camp-out, Bobby awoke in a very cheery mood. Kenny's dad came out and started a fire. Then he ran an extension cord to a plug-in griddle, and Kenny's mom made pancakes for the boys while they warmed themselves by the fire.

Bobby sat smiling and very politely said "thank you," to everything that was handed to him or done for him.

Kenny watched him closely, not recognizing the boy who woke up in the tent with him. This Bobby wasn't the bully he once was, but he had also lost his sad, angry edge.

"Hey Bobby," Kenny's mom said. "You know Thanksgiving is coming up in just a couple weeks?"

Bobby had just taken a bite of pancakes and swallowed them quickly. "Yeah."

"We were wondering if you and your father wanted to join us for dinner?"

Bobby turned and looked up at her. "My dad?" he said as if trying to register what he'd heard.

"Yes," she smiled back at him.

"Ummm," Bobby looked back at Kenny, and he began to bounce one foot. "I can ask him."

"Great. You do that. We'd love to have you both with us." She poured more batter on the griddle and hummed while she cooked.

Bobby looked up at her, his cheery expression now turned contemplative. He sat back in his chair and stared at the fire, still bouncing his foot. Kenny watched him take another bite of pancakes and chew slowly. He didn't know much about Bobby's mom or why she left, but he suspected that Bobby missed her.

After breakfast, the boys helped pack up the tent and clean up the backyard. Bobby was back to a lighter mood and thanked Kenny's mom and dad before heading home on his bike.

"I've never seen him in such a good mood," Kenny said.

His mother rubbed the top of his head. "You've been good for him." She squeezed his shoulder. "And hasn't he been good for you, too?"

Kenny shrugged. "I guess." He thought about it. It was good to have a friend but being with Bobby hadn't changed *his* entire personality.

The next day, Kenny's dad drove him to school and parked the car. He walked in with Kenny and talked to Mr. Fenstamaker about what had occurred on Saturday night in the backyard with Tunney, Gable, and Sawyer. Although it didn't happen on school grounds, Mr. Fenstamaker had a big problem with bullying. He called all the boys into his office, along with their parents.

Kenny didn't know exactly what happened, but the three never bothered them again. They didn't even give them so much as a mean look.

When Bobby stopped by after school, Kenny's mom

asked him if he'd talked to his dad about Thanksgiving.

"Yeah," Bobby said. "He said he guessed so."

"He guessed so?"

"Yes. And he said to say, thank you."

Kenny's mom smiled and nodded. "Okay. We'll see the two of you on Thanksgiving then."

The two boys were practically inseparable in the two weeks leading up to Thanksgiving. Kenny was focused on making sure that Bobby understood arithmetic, and Bobby wanted to get Kenny ready for the Paralympics coming up in Arnhem.

Bobby's scores on quizzes were seeing improvement, and though Kenny wouldn't be ready for the 100-yard dash any time soon, he could certainly move faster. He was almost up to what one might consider a jog.

But their favorite pastime was still playing Pong in the basement. "You boys need to spend as much time outside as you can." Kenny's mom would say. "You'll have all winter to play that silly game."

At one point, Kenny's dad surprised him with a set of walkie-talkies. When his mom complained about it, he told her it was a way to get them out of the basement.

The boys found the walkie-talkies fun for a while. They would ride their bikes up different blocks of the neighborhood and tell each other what they were seeing. When they realized the great distance they could communicate, the walkie-talkies became more of a tool for communication than a toy to play with. Nearly every night, when they were both supposed to be going to sleep, Bobby and Kenny would pull them out from under their beds and talk to each other until they were too tired.

At first, it was simply fun to talk just because they knew they were getting away with something. Then they talked about which girls were cute in school, and movies and TV shows. Kenny would sometimes take the opportunity to make sure that Bobby was ready for the following day's arithmetic quiz.

But eventually, they would lie there, heads on their pillows staring at the dark ceiling or the moonlight in the window and talk about life.

"Can I ask you something?" Kenny said.

"Sure," Bobby said, followed by the hiss and the snap of the walkie-talkie speaker.

Kenny pushed the button. "Promise you won't get mad?" Then he released the button.

"Okay." Hiss-snap.

"I've always wondered why your mom left. But I've been too afraid to ask." Kenny figured that if he was going to ask the question, now was the time when they were separated by a block and a half. But when there was only silence, he realized he should have never said anything. He pushed the button again. "I'm sorry. It's not my business. I'm sorry."

There was still no answer. "Bobby?"

"Yeah," Hiss-snap.

"I'm sorry."

"It's okay. I guess I just still get sad whenever I think about it."

"Don't worry about it. Did you see *Land of the Lost* last weekend?" Kenny felt bad and wanted to get to something else quick so he could take Bobby's mind off it.

There was a long pause before Bobby said. "She left because my dad was always so mean to her. She couldn't take it anymore."

"Why was he so mean to her?"

"Because he's a mean guy."

"Does he drink too much?" Kenny had heard his dad talk to his mom one time about people who could be mean drunks. That was the only explanation he could think of.

"No. Not then," Bobby said. "That didn't really start until after she left. He's just a...a butthead, I guess."

"Do you still get to talk to her?"

"Yeah. She calls me every once in a while."

Kenny thought he'd heard Bobby's voice crack. It sounded like Bobby may have started to cry. He instantly regretted bringing it up at all, and now he really wanted to change the subject.

He pushed the button. "Hey, Bobby. Did you see *Land of the Lost* last weekend? The Sleestaks are the scariest things ever invented."

There was a long pause before Bobby came back on. "I'm tired now. Goodnight, Kenny." Hiss-snap.

"Bobby?" Kenny didn't want him to sign off. Not like that. But there was no answer, and he knew there would be nothing more coming. He pushed the button one more time. "Good night." Then he turned the knob on the side until it clicked off and slid the walkie-talkie back under his bed.

He laid there looking out the window, thinking about what Mr. Fenstamaker had said to Bobby on Field Day—that he was just like Kenny because he'd lost something, too. He'd lost his mom and Kenny had lost his leg. Kenny wondered if everybody who'd ever lost something important were exactly alike and if there was a name for them. Kenny had been labeled "handicapped." But what did you call someone who had lost their mom—*family-capped*?

Edwards

17

Wednesday before Thanksgiving

Margo hardly said a word during the entire drive to Cincinnati—I mean other than, "Can you drive through a Starbucks?" and "Can you stop at the next rest area?"

I knew she wasn't happy about heading off to Bobby Booker's funeral the day before Thanksgiving, but she was so concerned about my health and welfare after the scare the previous day, she was not going to say no. If it was something I felt I needed to do, she was going to support me. But there was no way she was going to let me go alone.

Isabel, thank goodness, had stepped in and offered to make the seven-layer-salad and the green bean casserole, two very essential Thanksgiving staples. She still wasn't happy with me for turning down her sister's loan, but apparently her ill feelings didn't extend to helping out due to the fact that I'd had a near-death experience.

We had to park down the street about a block and a half

because we were running behind and the parking lot of the Fremont and Moore Funeral Home was completely full.

"Do you think all these cars are for him?" Margo said.

I shrugged. "One way to find out."

When we reached the funeral home I noticed a hearse under an awning, ready and waiting to take Bobby to his forever sleep.

A gentleman in a dark suit greeted us when we entered and gestured to a large, crowded room to our left.

My eyes were instantly drawn to Bobby, lying in his mahogany casket at the front of the room, surrounded by a forest of flowers. The lush reds, bright yellows, stunning oranges, pinks, and whites made it look sad, peaceful, and beautiful, all at the same time.

Margo squeezed my hand and whispered to me. "Ken, are you seeing this?"

When I looked around the room I was struck, not only by the number of people that showed up for a funeral but by the make-up of the crowd. A woman in front of me wore a black dress that came down to her knees—or should I say knee. One leg was prosthetic. She was talking to another woman and a man, both with prosthetic arms. As I looked at the small clusters of people gathered together talking, the vast majority of them had prosthetic arms, legs, or hands. Never in my life had I ever seen a crowd where a full-bodied individual was a rarity.

And then I realized that I had never been in a room where I was the one who fit in with everyone else, and Margo was the one who was different.

"You made it!"

I recognized Dawn Booker's voice and turned to greet her. She appeared genuinely happy to see me. Behind her was a young woman, who smiled at us sadly but politely.

"I'm so happy to see you." Dawn gave me a warm hug and when I introduced her to Margo, she hugged her, too. Then she introduced us to their daughter, Lila.

After all of the introductions, I broached the subject of all of the people with prosthetics in attendance.

"It's what he did for a living," she said. "He was a physical therapist specializing in amputee rehabilitation."

"You're kidding me," I said. I think my jaw dropped down to at least the third button on my shirt.

"No." Dawn shook her head. "And it's because of *you*. After what you did for him, he felt he owed it to you. He wanted to give back to you and the amputee community." She reached up and squeezed my arm. "That's why I'm so glad you made it today. Everyone here knows about you and your story." Then she hooked my arm and dragged me into the room. "Come on. They'll be blown away to finally meet the real Kenny Pritchard."

I reached over and grabbed Margo's hand and pulled her along with us.

Dawn brought us over to an older gentleman who was talking to two middle-aged women.

"Hi, Lonnie. Sorry to interrupt, but I want you to meet someone." She pulled me in. "This is Mr. Kenny Pritchard."

All three sets of eyes practically bugged out of their heads. One of the women put her prosthetic hand on her heart and cried out, "Oh my gosh." The other one just put her human hand over her mouth. And the man named Lonnie said. "Well, I'll be damned." He held out his hand. "Lonnie Arnolds."

I was so stunned by all of the fanfare, it took me a moment to realize he wanted to shake my hand. When I finally took it, I said. "*Ken*. Ken Pritchard. Nice to meet you."

"Oh, Ken. Not Kenny," Dawn laughed. "Sorry about that."

"No problem," I said, and then introduced Margo.

Both women shook my hand and Margo's. Their names were May and Abby.

"We all have three things in common," May said. "We've all lost a limb, we all had Bobby Booker as our rehab specialist, and we've all heard of you."

"Lonnie was Bobby's very first patient," Dawn said.

"That's right." Lonnie lifted his right pant leg to show his prosthetic—a metal bar that went down into his shoe. He dropped the pant leg and looked up at me. "And Bobby told your story to me on the very first day I met him."

The two women nodded. "Us too," Abby said. "What you did, changed his life."

The man who greeted us at the front door walked up to Dawn, "Mrs. Booker, it's time."

Dawn's smile faded and she nodded. She leaned into me. "Can I ask one more thing of you?"

"Sure. What do you need?" I said. I had a professor in college who told me never to say yes to a request until I knew exactly what was being asked of me.

"Would you be willing to stand up and say a few words for Bobby?"

That professor was never wrong. "But these people know Bobby better than I did."

"But if not for you, these people would not even be here," Dawn said. "You changed his whole life."

I realized I couldn't say no to a grieving widow. I nodded, and she squeezed my arm once more. "Thank you."

She turned to her daughter, they took each other's hand, and walked to their seats in the front of the room, stopping first to talk to the funeral director.

He nodded at her and then stepped up to the front of the room near Bobby's casket and spoke to the crowd. "We're going to get started. If you could all find a seat, please."

"It was a real honor to meet you, Ken," Lonnie said.

"Yes, it was," Abby said.

"Thank you so much for coming today," May said. Then all three of them walked off to take a seat.

Margo leaned in and whispered in my ear. "It's crazy that all these people have heard of you. What exactly did you do for this man?"

I was feeling a little overwhelmed by all the attention. "Nothing really." I searched for a seat, found two still open, and sat down with Margo, still clutching her hand tightly.

Once everyone had taken their seat, the man stepped up to the lectern in front and thanked us all for coming to celebrate the life of Bobby Booker.

"Dawn and I talked," he said. "And we decided it was best, and quite appropriate actually, to start the ceremony off with Bobby's favorite song."

"Oh no," I whispered.

"From what I understand, he has played this song for many of you during your time with him. Think of him again as you listen to it now." The man nodded to someone in the back and the music began. It was *I'm Still Standing*, one of Elton John's. I loved that song. I thought it was also very appropriate and I was very glad his musical taste had improved. The song seemed to lighten the mood. Like it truly *was* a celebration of Bobby now.

Once it ended the funeral director stepped back up to the lectern and looked down at the sheets of paper in front of him.

"The great Jackie Robinson once said, 'A life is not important except in the impact it has on other's lives.'" He looked up at the crowd. "It seems that he and Bobby shared that same sentiment. Most of you in this room met Bobby at, quite possibly, the worst moment in your lives. You didn't know him at that point. He was just the next person in line to care for you as an amputee. But you quickly came to realize he was different. He cared about what you were going through, and he was driven to help you overcome what you felt was a horrible, disfiguring disability." He paused and scanned the crowd, then looked back down at his papers. "I could stand here for quite a while and tell you all of the things I've learned about Bobby in the past few days. He loved his wife, Dawn, and his daughter, Lila, with all of his heart. Pretzels were his go-to snack food, and Thanksgiving was his favorite holiday." He held up the paper. "I have lists of Bobby Booker trivia, but that's not really what we're here for today. We're here to celebrate who he was, and the impact he had on everyone in this room. So, I'm going to cede the lectern to anyone who wants to come up and speak, to briefly tell the story of what Bobby did for you."

He put up a finger. "But first I have another quote. This one is from an anonymous source. 'Sometimes people come into your life for a moment, a day, or a lifetime. It matters not the time they spent with you, but how they impacted your life in that time.' So, before I open the mic to you all, I'd like to bring up a man who, though he was only in Bobby's life briefly in their youth, his impact on Bobby lasted a lifetime—Mr. Kenny Pritchard."

There were audible gasps in the room when my name was called. I looked over to Margo for some source of encouragement, and she didn't let me down. She gave me her patented wink and smirk that said, "Go get'em, Tiger." That was everything I needed.

I stood and walked up the side of the room, painfully aware of the necks that were craning to get a glimpse of me. I don't think I've felt that awkward since I walked to school on the first day of fifth grade with my brand-new prosthetic leg.

When I reached the front, I stopped and took a moment to look at my old friend lying in his casket. His face, though now made up, still looked incredibly gaunt. His eyes were sunk deep into his skull. His hands across his chest looked thin and feeble. It was sad to see, knowing that he'd been such a strong man in life.

I turned to the podium and looked out into the many faces that were here for Bobby. Young faces, old faces, black, white, and brown faces. Every hair color under the sun, including a few that I didn't know even existed. These were all Bobby's people. He helped them—turned their entire lives around. And they looked up at me now, smiling through their pain. They seemed expectant as if I held the secrets to everything Bobby Booker. Maybe they wanted me to regale them with our vast history together.

I never felt phonier than at that moment.

Then my eyes landed on one single solitary person—an old gentleman sitting in a wheelchair off to the side near the back. He had surrendered his height, strength, and stature to age, but something about him still demanded respect. Mr. Fenstamaker looked up at me with a smile and gave me a proud nod.

I realized at that moment, that it wasn't Bobby who had brought everyone together—it was Mr. Fenstamaker. He was the man whose genius put all of this in motion. *He* had made the decision that changed everyone's life in this room.

That realization meant I actually did have secrets to tell. But I also knew that if I told those secrets it would take away from what we were here for, and that was to celebrate Bobby Booker.

Finally, I got up the nerve to open my mouth. "Hi," I said, and then cleared my throat.

"Hi, Kenny," someone in the back said, and the room rumbled with subdued laughter.

I smiled. "I actually go by Ken now."

The laughter returned, a little louder.

I sighed and said, "I'm actually surprised that anybody here even knows my name, let alone the fact that I've been asked to be the first speaker. My guess is that the majority of you probably spent more time in Bobby's life than I did." I looked back at Bobby. "I would be lying if I said that we were friends from the very first time we met."

There were chuckles from the crowd. I looked out at them. "Did he tell you all that he used to bully me?" Many of them nodded. I looked over at Mr. Fenstamaker, who was still smiling. "And then one day, he became my bodyguard, and before you knew it, he was my best friend…and the rest is history."

I took a breath and tried my best to look each of them in the eye. "Bobby was strong, loyal, and he believed in me until I could finally see what he believed in." I chuckled. "I never did make it to the Paralympics though."

Laughter erupted at that statement. I looked around the room at everyone looking at each other like they were in on the joke. "Oh no. You too?" They looked up at me with smiles and I now felt at ease. Bobby's people were all good people, and they accepted me.

When it quieted back down, I started again, sounding as solemn as I now felt. "I understand Bobby told you about our Thanksgiving a hundred years ago, and he probably made it all sound very dramatic and grandiose. But the truth is, I didn't do anything he wouldn't have done for me, or any of you wouldn't have done. But I think what made it special to him is that it was the first time anybody stepped up in his life. I'm happy to be here and see that hasn't changed. If I have a regret, it's that I didn't keep in touch with Bobby as I should have. After seeing you all, I now realize how much richer my life would have been."

I looked at the two tortured faces in the front row. "Dawn. Lila. Thank you for asking me here today. I'm so very sorry for your loss." Then I turned back. "And Bobby. I haven't seen or talked to you in years, and now I feel like I'm going to miss you forever."

I looked back at the crowd, specifically Mr. Fenstamaker, and said, "Thank you."

The old man gave me another proud nod.

When I made it back and sat down next to Margo, she smiled at me through tears and then kissed me lightly on the cheek.

I sat back and listened to the flood of people walk up to the lectern and tell how Bobby made them feel the first time they met him. How he always encouraged them, supported them, called them on weekends to make sure they were doing their exercises. Bobby made himself a fixture in

140

their lives and didn't let up until they were successful, self-sufficient, and could sing the Elton John song and genuinely believe it. And then, somehow they remained in touch, friends for life after that.

I tried very hard, as I took it all in, to find a correlation in my own life. Did I have one friend, one acquaintance, one client who felt the same devotion to me? And what kind of passion did I have for my job—had I been kidding myself all these years that I was helping people, except, of course, when they were deserving but didn't have the collateral

Once in a while, I would look over and catch Margo staring at me. She would turn away when I caught her.

When the funeral portion finished and the casket taken out to the hearse, people stood in line to say goodbye to Margo and me. They were disappointed that we weren't staying for lunch, and quite honestly I was disappointed then too, but I had promised Margo we would leave to get things ready for Thanksgiving.

Dawn and Lila both gave us long, warm hugs, and we promised to keep in touch.

Then I made my way over to Mr. Fenstamaker who sat off to one side with, what I assumed was his son. "It's very great to see you, sir," I said. "Thank you for all that you did for Bobby and me."

Mr. Fenstamaker looked up at me and smiled, his old, yellowed teeth having lost their alignment. "In all the years I worked in education, I never had a success that ever came close to you and Bobby. You two were the bar I set that I could never reach again. I'm very proud of you, Kenny."

"Thank you," I said, and we parted ways knowing we would never see each other on this earth again. My thoughts went to my father, and I wondered how he was getting along. I probably should have stopped by to check on him before heading to the funeral.

I walked Margo back to the car, opened the door for her, and then got in on my side. I was just about to start it when she said, "Wait."

I looked over at her. "What's up?"

"In all the years I've been married to you, you've never mentioned the name Bobby Booker. Now I learn that you did this incredible thing that made an unbelievable impact in his life, so much so, that he's told everyone else he ever knew about it. Now I've sat patiently through an entire funeral wondering what it is that you've kept from me all this time, and we're not going anywhere until I hear it!"

18

Thanksgiving Day
Back in the Day

Thanksgiving Day had finally arrived, and the Pritchard house was getting ready. The turkey was in the oven, and mom and dad were busy preparing the rest of the food.

They had put an insert in the table to make it bigger, placed a brown tablecloth over it and Kenny set the table with two extra plates on one side for Bobby and Mr. Booker. His mom came by after him and straightened everything out. Then she sat a centerpiece in the middle that she had made out of sunflowers and cornstalks. When she was done, the table looked elegant.

The Detroit Lions were playing the Los Angeles Rams and Kenny's dad had taken over the TV, so Kenny went downstairs to kill time by playing Pong against the computer until Bobby got there at 4:30. But 4:40 came around and there was still no Bobby. Kenny decided to run up to his bedroom and try to see if he could contact him on the walkie-talkie. No luck.

He walked back out to the kitchen. "When is Bobby going to get here?"

"They're only a few minutes late," his mom said. "But if you want, you can put your coat on and ride your bike down there to see how they're coming along."

Kenny decided it was better than just sitting around and waiting, so he put on his down jacket, and stocking cap and got his bike out of the garage.

Holidays in his neighborhood were always fascinating to Kenny. Any day of the week, the place was busy. There were always cars driving by, people outside doing yard work, or kids playing. But on days like Thanksgiving, it was like all life ceased to exist. Nobody was outside. They were all inside eating and relaxing.

Kenny reached Bobby's house, which was just as quiet as every other house in the neighborhood. He parked his bike in the driveway and headed to the front door. He was almost to the porch when the front door opened. He heard Bobby's voice say, "...already late."

And then the much louder gruff voice of Mr. Booker said, "I already said, you can't be late if you're not going."

"But we told them we'd go. And I want to."

"Get back here and close that door."

"No. You can stay here and drink all day if you want to, but I'm going."

The screen door opened and Bobby started to emerge from the house, but before he noticed Kenny standing there, a large hand reached out, grabbed his messy hair, and yanked him back in.

"I said, *no!*" His father growled, and then Kenny heard a crash. There were the distinct sounds of snapping wood and broken ceramic. He froze, rooted in the spot, not knowing what to do.

He heard Bobby crying. "Why you gotta do this?"

"Why you gotta run off on Thanksgiving?" Mr. Booker

howled.

"But you told them we were going."

"I changed my mind. Do you have a problem being together as a family?"

Bobby screamed at his dad. "But we're *not* a family. Mom left us because of *you*."

Then came the unmistakable sound of a slap, and Bobby cried out.

Kenny hurried to the porch and tried his best to see through the screen. Bobby was lying on the floor in a heap next to a broken lamp, his arm covering his face while he cried.

"How *dare* you say that to me," Mr. Booker said, in a low angry growl. He reached down grabbed Bobby by the front of his shirt and lifted him off the ground. "She left here because she couldn't take your endless whining anymore." With a balled-up fist, he struck Bobby across the face. Bobby's head snapped backward.

Kenny cried out, and threw his hands over his mouth, surprised by his own outburst. He ran back toward his bike but stopped. His heart was thumping in his chest, and his hands were shaking. His mind was racing but he knew he needed to slow down and think. He couldn't ride away and just leave Bobby. What if Mr. Booker killed him?

He heard a door open across the street, and he saw Mr. Pemberton let in their cat. "Hey! Wait!" Kenny called. But Mr. Pemberton closed the door.

Kenny ran down the driveway and out into the street. It was when he reached the Pemberton's driveway that he realized he really was running. All that time Bobby had spent working with him was now paying off, for Bobby's own sake. It was weird how things worked out sometimes.

Kenny bolted up the porch of the Pemberton house and started pounding on the door, and ringing the bell.

In a moment the door swung open and an angry-looking Mr. Pemberton filled the doorway. "What are you doing!"

he snapped.

"Call the police!" Kenny pointed toward the Booker house. "I think he's going to kill Bobby."

Mr. Pemberton looked across the street. "What are you saying?"

"Mr. Booker is beating up Bobby." Kenny was starting to cry.

Mr. Pemberton shook his head. "Kid, I can't call the police if a parent wants to spank his boy."

Just then, the screen door of the Booker house swung open and Bobby stumbled out. Even at that distance, you could tell his nose was bleeding. There was blood all over his face and down the front of his shirt. Mr. Booker ran out, grabbed Bobby by the coat, and threw him back into the house.

"Holy crap!" Mr. Pemberton said. "Ellen, call 9-1-1 and have them get to the Booker house now!" He opened the door for Kenny. "You need to come in here and wait, kid."

But Kenny didn't wait. For the first time in seven months, Kenny sprinted. With his new leg he darted up Bobby's driveway, up the walk and this time didn't stop at the porch. Something about seeing Bobby, beaten and bloody, and then thrown back into the house like a doll had emboldened Kenny. All he could hear was Bobby's voice in his head, "Can't you ever fight back?" He honestly didn't know if he could or not, but for Bobby's sake, this time he was going to try.

Kenny threw open the screen door to see Bobby on the floor with Mr. Booker on top of him. Mr. Booker was swinging at his face, and shouting, "It was *you*. It was *you*." Bobby had his arms over his face, trying to defend himself and screaming.

For a moment, Kenny watched in horror not knowing what to do. He looked around. A small table near the TV had been smashed, and a lamp had fallen on the floor broken. There were empty beer cans crowded around an ashtray on a table next to a La-Z-Boy chair. The ashtray was full of cigarette butts, but it was big. It was made of wood, in the shape of the state of Ohio, and it had a big glass insert. All Kenny cared about was that it looked heavy. When he grabbed it, the contents fell out in a putrid cloud of ash. He ran over and stood behind Mr. Booker and shouted, "Stop!"

Mr. Booker, startled by the noise, jerked himself around in time for the heavy ashtray to collide with the side of his head. He fell off Bobby, onto a small wooden coffee table, crushing it under his weight, and lay there motionless.

Kenny stared at the scene. Realizing what he'd just done, he stopped breathing.

"What did you do?" Bobby said. He sat up, blood still running from his nose and a cut on his lip, and he crawled away from his dad backward on all fours.

Kenny's hands were shaking and he dropped the ashtray. It landed with a clunk, leaving a dent in the wood flooring.

Mr. Booker moaned and rubbed his head.

"You have to get out of here," Bobby said, scrambling to his feet. "He's going to kill you."

Bobby grabbed Kenny, whose feet were moving so fast just moments before, but were now completely unable to even take a step.

"Come on, Kenny," Bobby dragged Kenny out the door and down the porch.

They both heard a loud angry howl from inside the house, and then the door opened so hard it practically blew off the hinges. Mr. Booker stood on the porch looking at them with blood-red eyes and the snarl of an angry bear. He lurched down the steps toward the boys,

Bobby was still dragging Kenny, who was now so terrified that he couldn't even think straight to take a step on his own.

Just before Mr. Booker reached them, another man flew past from the other direction. Mr. Pemberton tackled Mr.

Booker and held him down. Mr. Booker struggled, kicked, and screamed, but it was no use. He was too drunk to really fight a grown-up, and Mr. Pemberton had at least a hundred pounds on him.

Within minutes, sirens could be heard and two police cars pulled to a stop in front of the house. They jumped out of their cars, guns drawn. Mr. Pemberton raised his arms and stood. Mr. Booker jumped from the ground and lunged toward Bobby, but the police tackled him, cuffed him, and shut him in the back seat of one of the police cars.

Kenny looked up at Bobby, and with tears in his eyes, he said, "I'm so sorry, Bobby."

"You're sorry?" Bobby said, wiping blood from his face. "Kenny, don't be sorry. You saved my life!"

19

Thanksgiving Day

Margo and I woke early on Thanksgiving Day to get things started. We got home late the previous night because we had spent the entire day talking.

Once the funeral had ended, she wouldn't let me start the car until I told her the whole horrible story about that Thanksgiving Day so long ago, and what I had done that still had everyone buzzing. When I said I could drive and talk at the same time she refused. She wanted to be able to look into my eyes and listen. So we compromised—I drove to an Italian restaurant and told her over lunch.

We ended up staying there for hours talking about Bobby, my life in fifth grade, even that night camping that was so good and yet bad at the same time.

"It all makes sense to me," Margo said, then devouring her last bite of tiramisu.

"What does?"

She put her fork down. "Bobby Booker and his chosen profession."

"Because he helped me ride a bike and run?"

"No." She washed her desert down with another sip of wine. "The only person who showed any concern for him in his life was an amputee. You were the only one who ever stood up for him. You put your own safety on the line, and he never forgot that. So, he became a rehab specialist to not only give back but to be with you. All his life he was chasing that same feeling you gave him that Thanksgiving Day."

Of course, Margo was right. I had just thought about his curious career choice in a different way—that he was fascinated by me, the science part of the prosthesis, and his goal for me to make the Paralympics.

By the time we were done, we had finished a whole bottle of wine and Margo didn't want me driving home right away. I ended up having pizzas delivered to the house for Amber, Casey, and Celine, and then we headed to the Cincinnati Zoo. We spent another few hours walking arm in arm, while we talked more. It wasn't about Bobby then, it was about life. Not just our life, but life in general. I did mention the incident that set off my heart episode and how nervous I was to see Monday come around. I wasn't sure what was going to happen at the board meeting.

Whether or not she was upset too, she didn't let it show. She never lost her smile. She just said, "That's days away. Let's not worry about it now. In fact, let's not worry about anything today. Let's just be together." And that's who Margo was to me. I could be completely vulnerable to her and she wouldn't judge me. She was genuinely happy to be with me. No other person on this planet had ever been like that. They all looked at a man with one leg and instantly saw limitations. I had to work harder than everyone to prove I was just like them. But not Margo. From the day I met her she never seemed to notice that I only had one leg. She always made me feel...whole.

It was great to escape life for a day and not worry about anything, but we were paying for it. We had to get up extra early on Thanksgiving morning to get the turkey ready and in the oven for dinner. We set to work, me cleaning the bird, and Margo making the stuffing. We worked in silence and not just because we were groggy from lack of sleep. We realized we couldn't run from life forever.

They give you all sorts of tips on managing stress and they all seem stupid to me. I can do deep breathing all day long, but that doesn't take away the fact that I have someone in my life who is determined to fire me.

We met at the counter and worked together stuffing the turkey, then I trussed it up, poured water and half a bottle of Pino Grigio in the pan, and got it in the oven to roast low and slow all day long.

It seemed like as soon as the oven door closed, Margo had a bottle of Bailey's in her hand. "Pour us some more coffee," she said. "I have a proposition I want to discuss with you."

"And I need to be drinking to hear it?" I said with a chuckle.

She didn't smile. She just nodded and said, "Ohhhh, yeah."

I got us our coffee and she poured in the Bailey's. Then we put on our coats and sat out in the now-chilly, three-seasons room. It was a great place in the spring and summer because it looked out on the beautiful gardens that Margo loved to maintain. But now there were mostly brown leaves that I had yet to rake up.

"How did it feel being there yesterday?" Margo asked me, as soon as our butts hit the seat.

"Ummm...sad?" I didn't know what she was getting at.

"No. Not because of Bobby. How did it feel being in a room full of amputees?"

"Oh," I actually hadn't given it much thought. It was strange to see that many people with prosthetics all gathered in one place, but I hadn't thought about it in terms of my feelings on it. "Kind of surreal, I guess." But then I thought about standing in front of them. And instead of feeling nervous speaking in front of a bunch of people I didn't know, I felt at ease, like...they were my tribe. "But I guess I also felt a comfort, too."

"How so?"

"Well, I've never been in a room that big with so many people that were just like me. I think there's a certain comfort in that."

"So, not stressed then?" Margo took a sip from her coffee which was steaming away in the cold.

"I was stressed when I went up to speak, but it went away quickly because they treated me like one of the family."

"Exactly," she said, smirking. "How would it be to feel like that every day?"

I was now lost. "What are you talking about?"

"What I'm talking about is you walking in on Monday and telling the board of directors to shove it. Quit your job and become a rehab specialist just like your friend Bobby Booker."

"Babe, I can't do that." This was not like Margo. She was usually pretty level-headed. "Just the other day we talked and you mentioned Amber's college and trip and..."

"Forget what I said. That was before I knew this job, this *life* was killing you." She took my hand. "And I'd much rather have you than anything else."

"But what about my community? Wouldn't I be letting them down?"

"Did Bobby Booker let them down?"

"Margo, this is silly. I can't just decide to become a rehab specialist and go get a job tomorrow. There's a great deal of training involved. And I'm too old to start a new career."

"I get that we'd have to go back to school, but that's what makes it even more exciting."

"We?"

Margo sat back and smiled. "Yes. I'm going to do it with you." She took a sip of her coffee.

I have to admit, just hearing that made the whole thing more attractive to me. But there were too many other problems with the plan. "We couldn't afford to live here, and Amber still has college and her trip to France and..."

"We're going to sell this place and get a much smaller one. We don't need a house this big anyway, and we can use the money to get started. Amber can go to community college her first two years, and she doesn't need to go to France again."

"And Casey?"

"Can get a real job."

"You've got this all figured out."

"I do."

I took a sip of my coffee, very happy now that it had the Bailey's in it. I was trying to process her plan in my head. I had to admit that if I were even ten years younger it would be a no-brainer, but to start school again and work toward a whole new career when I was approaching fifty, seemed borderline insane.

"And why would I do this instead of going back to a bank manager position? I could just ride out my last years in that role and retire."

Margo shrugged. "Yes. That's an option. It's just not a good option. If you were to go back to being a bank manager it would look bad—like you failed. But by picking a whole new career to ride out your working life, especially one that supports your community, you actually look like a hero. Plus, you would get to work with me every single day at our brand-new facility."

"New facility?"

"Yep."

"We're starting our own rehab facility?"

She nodded, smiling wide. "We'll get it started right

away and hire a few top-notch rehab specialists. I've researched this. Since we already have degrees, we could be licensed therapists within three years and then work there, too. Meanwhile, you run the place. You can go back to school with me or just be the boss, either is fine." She winked. "You see, you're something of a big deal. With your name attached to the business, it's bound to be incredibly successful."

I laughed. Margo was nothing if not someone who had big dreams. She was also tenacious enough to make them happen. And this was a great opportunity to use her marketing degree. It sounded like she'd already started.

She took my hand again. "Ken, if you tell me that this is a stupid idea and have no interest in doing something like this, I will drop the whole thing and let you figure things out. But after what happened on Tuesday, I got scared. Nothing is worth losing you. And I watched you closely the entire time we were at Bobby's funeral. There was peace and contentment in your eyes, and I think it had to do with being around people like you. I realized I wanted to see that look every single day. And I think you'd find it rewarding. There's very good energy and personal satisfaction that comes from helping others."

Her dream sounded amazing. And to be honest, Tuesday shook me up, too. It made the whole crazy scheme sound more palatable. I just had to stop the voices in my head that told me it was wrong and wouldn't work. I've had them in my head all my life. It was usually Margo who helped me silence them. "Can I think about it?"

"Absolutely."

We finished our coffee in silence, holding hands and watching the breeze blow the leaves around in the backyard. Then we went in and started cooking the Thanksgiving feast.

A large bouquet of flowers had been delivered to the house on Tuesday evening with a card that read, "Our best wishes for a speedy recovery." It was signed, "The Board of Directors, Ohio Continental Bank."

Margo took the flowers into the kitchen, ripped the card into shreds, and completely dismantled the entire bouquet. Then she fashioned an amazing centerpiece using a few selected flowers and greenery.

In the early afternoon, I drove over and picked up my father so he could watch the Lions game with Casey and me. He wasn't in a great mood. He still had a large bandage on his forehead and was moving rather gingerly. In the car, on the way back I told him all about Margo's plan for the rest of my life and asked him what he thought about it.

"If it makes you happy, then do it."

And that was the big question. Would I be happy starting my life all over again in a totally new and completely foreign direction?

After the Lions pulled off a stunner against the Packers, we sat down to eat. Everything tasted amazing as usual, and Margo mentioned that the next Thanksgiving table would have a highchair next to it.

That had gotten me thinking, where would that next Thanksgiving table be? Would it be in this house? Would it even be this table? It wasn't likely. Even if I didn't quit or get fired on Monday, Carl would have me out within the year.

I realized I could actually feel my stress level rise when thoughts of work crept back into my head. It was palpable, like someone had turned a switch to make my stomach lurch, and my heart beat a little faster. I felt anxious, then angry, and by the time the pecan and pumpkin pies were brought to the table, I had made a decision. "I have something to say."

Everyone stopped their chatter and looked up at me. I was on the spot now and there was no turning back. "My life...our life is going to change immensely." I looked over at Margo and her eyes lit up. It looked like she was going to burst out of her skin. I smiled at her. "On Monday I'm going to resign from my job and your mother and I are going to be working on opening our own physical rehab clinic."

Margo let out a yelp, that if you didn't know she was excited, you would have thought she'd broken her femur. She leaped from her chair threw her arms around me and gave me a kiss. "I'm so proud of you."

"Wait," Amber said. "What does this mean?"

Margo sat back down and did the explaining for me. "It means we have to tighten our budget. We will be selling this house and downsizing." She looked at Casey and Celine. "You will have to move out, so Casey, you have to find a job, even if it's a cashier job at Kroger until something better comes along."

"Hold. Wait." Amber said. "Remember, I have my last trip to France this year, and college next fall."

"Those won't be able to happen, dear," Margo said. She was taking it all on for me. She wasn't going to let me be stressed about anything ever again. "But you will be able to start community college in the fall."

"But that's not *fair*?" Amber's voice was so high I thought it was going to shatter the wine glasses.

"You know what?" Margo said. "Amber you're right. It's not fair. Thank you for saying something." She turned to me. "Ken, we didn't think about how unfair this was to Amber."

"Thank you," Amber said.

"So you'll have to continue working at the job that's killing you. I know it means you may quite possibly be dead of a heart attack by the end of the year. But that doesn't matter. Amber will be without her dad for the rest of her life, but she absolutely needs her week in France this summer." Margo looked back at Amber.

Amber dropped her fork and stood. "Nice." Then she stormed off to her room.

Casey broke the awkward silence left by her departure.

156

"I think it's a great idea."

"You do?" Margo and I said together.

"Yes." He nodded and looked at Celine. "In fact, I'd love to join you if you'd let me."

"You would?" we said together again.

"How does Pritchard and Son, Physical Rehabilitation sound?" He said with a chuckle.

Celine took his hand and smiled at him. "That sounds great," she said.

Margo and I looked at each other, both our mouths were hanging open. Neither of us was expecting to hear that, and we started laughing at the same time.

For better or worse, this was going to happen.

Edwards

20

Thanksgiving Day
Back in the Day

Kenny stood with his parents, and at least half of the neighborhood, and watched the scene. An ambulance had arrived and they had Bobby lying on a gurney while they cleaned his face, took his blood pressure, and shined a light in his eyes.

Kenny's dad had sat with him on the curb while he talked to a policeman about everything he'd seen and heard. Kenny was crying because he thought he was going to be in trouble for hitting Mr. Booker. But the officer thanked him for being brave enough to help his friend.

Now Kenny just wondered what was going to happen. It looked like Bobby's dad was going to go to jail. If that happened, who would take care of Bobby?

The question didn't linger long. A police officer walked up to them and spoke to his parents. "I just got word that we located the boy's mother. The ambulance will take him to the hospital and make sure he's okay, and she'll meet us there and pick him up."

"Is she going to be living here then?" Kenny asked.

"No, sir. I'm afraid not," the officer said. "Bobby will be going to live with his mom in Cincinnati."

"Cincinnati? *No*." Kenny started crying. He turned and grabbed his dad's arm. "Can Bobby come live with us? Please? Please? Please?"

His mom turned and ran back toward their house.

His dad knelt next to him and looked him in the eye. "It doesn't work like that, Kenny. Bobby has a mom who loves him, and he is going to go live with her now."

"She *doesn't* love him," Kenny screamed. "She left him. Why does she get him back now?"

"Because that's the way life works." His dad said.

Kenny leaned into his father and cried. He'd truly disliked Bobby just a couple of months ago, but now trying to think of life without him was unbearable. His father held him tight while he wailed.

After a few minutes, the officer came back over. "Hey, Kenny. They're going to put Bobby in the ambulance and take him to the hospital. Did you want to say goodbye to him before they do?"

Kenny pulled himself away from his dad, wiped his eyes and nose with the sleeve of his coat, and nodded.

"Wait," his mom cried out. She ran back up to Kenny, completely out of breath, and handed him a picture. "Here. Give this to Bobby. It's for him."

Kenny took the photo from her and looked at it. It was the picture of the two of them in the tent. The officer touched his shoulder lightly and guided him over to where Bobby lay on the cot. The paramedics and police all stood back to let the two boys have their moment.

Kenny handed him the picture. "This is for you."

"Thanks." Bobby looked at it and smiled. Then he

looked up at Kenny. "My mom's coming up."

Kenny could see that Bobby was happy about the news. He knew he had to be happy for his friend as well. "I heard," he said, but he didn't think it sounded as happy as it probably should have. It was very hard to sound happy when you were very, very sad.

"She's going to take me to live in Cincinnati with her," Bobby said. He didn't look so happy about that.

"I heard that too." Kenny didn't care that he didn't sound happy that time.

"I'm not sure the walkie-talkies will reach that far," Bobby said. "But the phone will."

"Uh-huh," Kenny said. But that wasn't enough. They wouldn't be able to walk to school together, ride bikes together, play Pong together, or anything anymore.

"I gotta tell you, that was probably the coolest thing anybody's ever done for me," Bobby said. "You know, taking on my dad like that."

Kenny didn't know what to say. He just muttered, "Uh-huh."

"I'm sorry I ever called you a loser, Kenny. You're not a loser. You're a complete hero. You helped us win field day, and you saved my life today. You're a winner, Kenny, and don't ever let anybody ever tell you any different. I'm sorry I said it."

"It's okay," Kenny said, and he couldn't help it, tears leaked from his eyes again.

Bobby sat up, wrapped his arms around Kenny tight and the two boys cried and hugged for several moments. "You're the best friend I've ever had," Bobby said.

"You too," Kenny squeaked out.

"I'm going to miss you," Bobby said.

"I'm going to miss you too," Kenny said.

When they finally released, Kenny stood back, and both boys wiped at their eyes. Several of the adults standing around were wiping their eyes too.

The paramedics swooped in, lifted Bobby's gurney off the ground, slid it in the back of the ambulance, and closed the doors. Then one of them turned to Kenny and said, "We'll take real good care of him, I promise."

Kenny watched the ambulance drive away. Somehow he knew he would never see Bobby again. There was a hole in him now. He knew it was made by sadness and he didn't know if it would ever be filled.

"Come on, buddy," His dad said, walking up to him and patting him on the shoulder. "Mom's got dinner ready. Let's go eat some turkey."

Kenny didn't think turkey was going to fill the hole. But he guessed he could give it a try.

21

Monday after Thanksgiving

I spent at least half the day on Sunday writing my letter of resignation to the board. I needed to have it done and over with while I still had the courage. It was all tucked away nicely in my laptop bag.

And then the news came on, the big story was about how the Fed was considering raising the interest rates, and the ripple effect it had on the stock market from just the simple fact they were discussing it. This meant two things. First, that I was right about the interest rates all along, and I had successfully protected the bank. And second, that Adam Akers was in trouble today.

I sat at the breakfast table in my shirt and tie for the last time, satisfied that I was going out as a winner.

Amber came into the kitchen and gave me a hug, and a kiss on the side of the head. "I'm proud of you," she said.

That was another stunner of sorts. Amber had come out

of her room on Sunday with a completely different outlook on things. She talked about how she had been struggling about deciding on a major in college. Up until then, she'd had no clue what to even do with her life. But now she too was interested in joining us in our new venture. Maybe she would even be in the same classes as Margo and me.

That cinched it. Not only was I working toward a life where I could make a difference to people who needed it, taking my whole family into that dream was the best thing that could have ever happened.

"Are we ready to go?" Margo asked. She was standing by the door with her coat on and boxes in her hand. She said she would be willing to go in and help me pack my office. It looked like she was definitely still into this crazy scheme.

I looked up at her and smiled. "That all depends. Did you call Isabel?"

"I did. Let's hit the road." She opened the door and walked out.

I had put my leg on before I sat down to breakfast so I was all ready to go. I stood, kissed Amber on the forehead, told her thanks, and to have a good day in school, grabbed my coat, and headed out the door.

"This is as exciting as it gets," Margo said on the way there. "For the first time in a long time, I feel alive, like we're really striving for something."

"I know what you mean," I said. "Having Amber on board has really taken away any indecision I may have had." There was something unique about heading toward this venture. It was one thing to be striving in my career and having Margo by my side as support. I had made it to the top. But now striving for something completely different and having Margo by my side as a partner, and the rest of my family along too. There was nothing that could ever stop us.

When we got to the bank, I took Margo's hand and walked her through the lobby. Seeing us walking in, both carrying empty boxes got everybody to stop and take a look. I paused at Steve Paxton's desk briefly. "Good morning, Steve. I wanted to let you know that Emilia Alejandro will be stopping by this morning. Could you keep an eye out for her and bring her straight up to my office when she arrives?"

"Ahhh, yessir," he said. He was the kind who was easily intimidated. That would have driven Bobby Booker crazy.

"And could you email me her info?"

"I'll get right on that."

"Thanks," I said, and continued with Margo to the elevators.

When we reached the tenth floor, Dianne greeted us with a couple of large Amazon boxes.

"Thank you for these," Margo said.

"Not a problem," Dianne said. And she gave me a big hug. "I'm glad you're all right, and I'm so happy for you guys." She turned to Margo. "He was always too good for this place."

Margo nodded. "I know it."

Margo and Dianne set to work packing up my office. They took my books off the shelves, pulled my diplomas and honorary degrees off the walls, as well as my awards and knick-knacks from side tables.

I sat at my desk, slipped my laptop into its dock, and began the paperwork for Emilia's business loan.

Margo picked up the picture of Bobby and me in the tent, with the blue ribbon stuck to the frame. She smiled and showed it to me. "This is going up in our lobby. There's going to be a frame next to it telling the story of you two."

Once her marketing engine had started, it just kept on revving.

They had the majority of the office cleared out when Steve Paxton and Emilia strode in. Steve looked around confused at the barren office. "Are you moving back to the corporate offices?"

"Nope," was the only response I gave him. I had Emilia's

papers done for the $50,000 loan she'd asked for. I copied all of the information over from her rejected forms. Dianne brought the printouts in and I had Emilia sign them right then.

"Wait, you're allowing this?" Paxton said.

"Yep," I said. "Probably one of the best investments this bank has ever made."

Emilia looked up at me and smiled. Then she signed the papers, turned them around to me and I signed them as well. Then I handed them to Steve and said, "Can you get the rest of this taken care of?"

"Ahhh, yessir," He took the papers from me and headed out the door.

Emilia came around the desk and gave me a big hug. "Thank you, so much."

"Just go make your dreams come true," I said.

She assured me she would and she followed Paxton out.

One hour later we were parked outside the corporate offices in Whitehall. And I was ready to march in and change the direction of my life.

"Do you need me to go with you?" Margo asked.

"No. I got this," I said.

She leaned in and gave me a kiss. Then she gave me that smile and wink. That was all the courage I needed. I grabbed the folder, got out of the car, and headed into the building.

Ellen, the building receptionist greeted me when I walked in. "Good morning, Mr. Pritchard. They're waiting for you."

"Thank you, Ellen."

I marched down the hall with purpose and passed through the double doors that led into the board room. All eleven board members were seated with my seat—the hot seat, being the only unoccupied chair in the room.

"Good morning, Ken." Carl Byers said. "I'm happy to

see you're doing better."

"Thank you, Carl," I said with a slight bow of my head. "I'm doing *much* better."

Sandy Haggerton spoke next. "The news this morning was quite a surprise. But we're all very happy with the decisions you've made."

"Thank you, Sandy."

"Aren't you going to have a seat?" Carl asked.

"No," I said. "I'll make this brief." I held up the folder. "This is my letter of resignation, effective immediately." I put it on the table and slid it down to Byers.

"Resignation?" said one of the board members named Jenkins. "Ken, why?"

"Because I don't take kindly to bullies." I looked directly at Carl. "I'm not going to be pushed around or intimidated. I would have happily worked here until retirement and made your bank even greater than it is now. But it has been made clear that my presence has not been wanted or appreciated. So I'm out."

All of the board members looked at Byers angrily. "Carl, is this is your doing?" Jenkins said.

Carl bit his lip and gave sidelong glances at everyone at the table. Then with a resigned sigh he looked back at me. "We could talk about renegotiating your contract?"

I smiled and shook my head. "As I said, the resignation was effective immediately, and that was a minute ago. I'm on my own time now, and I don't intend to spend any of it amongst you people." I gave them all a quick nod. "Good day, ladies and gentlemen." Then I turned and closed the doors on my way out.

As I walked down the hall I heard raised voices coming from the board room. I couldn't help but chuckle.

"Good day, Ellen," I said as I passed her again.

Ellen looked up at me a little confused. "Good day, Mr. Pritchard."

I stepped out of the building into the cool November

air. The sun peered out from under thick gray clouds for the first time in days and I felt free.

Walking back to the car and my waiting co-worker, I thought about what had transpired over the last week. The plain and simple truth of it was, all of this was due to Bobby Booker. He had changed my life as a youth, and now again as an adult, somehow injecting me with large doses of courage each time. Oddly enough, both times they came at Thanksgiving.

I realized that when the day came, and I was lying in my bed waiting to take my last breath, when I looked at all the people who've held strong and important influence over my life, Bobby's name would be near the top of the list—right under Margo's of course.

I had to get home and let Amber know I had an answer to her question. What am I thankful for? I'm thankful I had someone like Bobby Booker in my life—my bully, my bodyguard, and my best friend, all in one.

I opened the door and climbed in.

"How did it go?" Margo asked.

"It went just fine," I said. "Let's get this new life going?"

She smiled and kissed me. Then I started the car and drove away.

Thanks for reading!

If you would, please take a moment and leave an honest review. Reviews are extremely helpful to authors. It would be greatly appreciated. Thank you very much!

For more information on upcoming books please stop by my web page, rob-edwards.net and sign-up for updates. I will be sending out a newsletter every few months. You can also connect with me on Facebook at **@robedwardsstoryteller**, on Instagram at **robedwardsstoryteller**, or on Twitter at **@robedwards5000**.

Acknowledgments

First of all I would like to thank my wife, Dayna, for whom, without her support and encouragement, these books would not come to fruition. She drinks her coffee alone in the morning and watches TV alone at night while I am off in front of my laptop putting the words in my head onto the page. And then she comes along and becomes my first beta-reader, my blurb writer, and my cover concept person. In fact the image on the back of the book is hers. I picked it because I felt it looked just like the sidewalk that Kenny and Bobby used to walk to and from school. Though I toned down the colors a great deal this is a spectacular shot. She has a great eye and takes beautiful pictures of the world around her. You can find more of her work on her Instagram account at @great_itude. Go ahead and check it out. You won't be disappointed.

I want to thank my incredible beta-readers and all of their invaluable input.

I would also like to thank the remarkable editing and input from Anne Stanton, and all the folks at Mission Point Press for their work and continued support.

From top to bottom, Michigan is a great state for writers!

Made in the USA
Middletown, DE
29 November 2021

53709882R00095